VOYAGER IN NIGHT

VOYAGER IN NIGHT

NIGHT

C.J. Cherryh

DAW BOOKS, INC.

DONALD A. WOLLHEIM, PUBLISHER

1633 Broadway, New York, NY 10019

DAW TRADEMARK REGISTERED
U.S. PAT. OFF. MARCA
REGISTRADA. HECHO EN U.S.A.

PRINTED IN U.S.A.

Chapter One

1,000,000 rise of terrene hominids

75,000 terrene ice age

35,000 hunter-gatherers

BC 9000 Jericho built

BC 3000 Sumer thriving

BC 1288 Reign of Rameses in Egypt

BC 753 founding of Rome

Trishanamarandu-kepta was < >'s name, of shape subject to change and configurations of consciousness likewise mutable. But *Trishanamarandu-kepta* within-the-shell kept alert against the threat of subversive alterations, for some of the guests aboard were unreliable in disposition and in sanity.

Concerning < >'s own mental stability, < > was reasonably certain. < > had a longer perspective than most and consequently held a different view of events. The chronometers which might, after so many incidents and so frequent transits into jumpspace, be subject to creeping inaccuracies, reported that the voyage had lasted more than 100,000 subjective ship-years thus far. This agreed with < >'s memory. Aberrations in both records were possible, but < > thought otherwise.

AD 1066 Battle of Hastings

AD 1492 Columbus

AD 1790 early Machine Age

AD 1800 Napoleonic Wars

AD 1903 Kitty Hawk

AD 1969 man on the moon

< > never slept. Some of the minds aboard might have seized control, given that opportunity, so < > managed < >'s body constantly, sometimes at a high level of mental activity, sometimes at marginal awareness, but < > never quite slept. Closest analogue to dreamstate, < > felt a slight giddiness during jumpspace transits. That was to be expected in a mind, even after long and frequent experience of such passages. < > leapt interstellar distances with something like sensual pleasure in the experience, whether the feeling came from the unsettling of < >'s mind or < >'s physical substance. Fear, after all, was a potent sensation; and all sensations were precious after so long a span of life.

< > traveled, that was what < > did.

< > set < >'s sights on whatever star was next and pursued it.

AD 2300: discovery of FTL

AD 2354: The Treaty of Pell

End of the Company Wars

Founding of the Alliance

1/10/55: colonization of Gehenna

Building of Endeavor

Another voyage began. Little *Lindy* moved up in the immense skeletal clutch of a Fargone loader into the cargo sling of the can-hauler *Rightwise,* while *Rightwise*'s lateral and terminal clamps moved slowly to fix *Lindy* in next to a canister of foodstuffs. She actually massed less than most of the constant-temp canisters *Rightwise* had slung under her belly, less than the chemicals and the manufacturing components destined for station use.

She was in fact nothing but a shell with engines, an unlovely, jerry-rigged construction; and the Lukowskis, the Viking-based merchanter family which owned *Rightwise,* having only moderate larceny in their hearts and a genuine spacers' sympathy for *Lindy*'s young owners, settled for the bonus Endeavor Station offered for the delivery of such ships and crews in lieu of *Lindy*'s freight, and took labor for the passage of the Murray-Gaineses themselves. *Rightwise* had muscle to spare, and *Lindy*'s bonus would clear two percent above the mass charge: the owners were desperate.

So *Rightwise* checked *Lindy*'s mass by Fargone records, double checked the dented, unshielded tanks that they were indeed empty for the haul, grappled her on and took her through jump to Endeavor—unlikely reprieve for that bit of scrap and spit which should long since have been sent to recycling.

AD 3/23/55

The Murrays and Paul Gaines arrived at Endeavor with the same hopes as the rest of the out-of-luck spacers incoming. Endeavor was a

starstation in the process of building, sited in the current direction of
Union expansion, in a rich (if unexportable) aggregation of ores. But
trade would come, extending outward to new routes. Combines and
companies would grow here. And the desperate and the ambitious
flocked in. There were insystem haulers, freighted in on jumpships,
among them a pair of moduled giant oreships, hauled in by half a
dozen longhaulers in pieces, reassembled at Endeavor, of too great
mass to have come in any other way. They were combine ships out of
Viking, those two leviathans, and they collected the bulk of the adver-
tised bonus for ships coming to Endeavor. There was a tanker from
Cyteen; a freighter from Fargone, major ships—while most of the
independent cold-haulers that labored the short station-belt run were
far smaller, patched antiquities that gave Endeavor System the eerie
ambiance of a hundred-year backstep in time. They were owned by
their crews, those ancient craft, some family ships, most the associa-
tion of non-kin who had gambled all their funds together on war
surplus and ingenuity.

And smallest and least came ships like the Murray-Gaineses' *Lindy,*
an aged pusher-ship once designed for nothing more complex than
boosting or slowing down a construction span or sweeping debris from
Fargone Station's peripheries, half a hundred years ago. They had
blistered her small hull with longterm lifesupport. A human form
jutted out of her portside like a decoration: an EVApod made of an old
suit. Storage compartments bulged outward at odd angles almost as
fanciful as the pod. Tanks were likewise jury-rigged on the ventral
surface, and a skein of hazardously exposed conduits led to the war-
salvage main engine and the chancy directionals.

No established station would have allowed *Lindy* registry even before the alterations. She had been scheduled for junk at Fargone, and
so had many of her parts, taken individually. But at Endeavor *Lindy*
was no worse than others of her size. She was rigged for light pros-
pecting in those several rings of ore-laden rock which belted Endeavor
System, feeding the refiner-oreships, which would send their recovered
materials in girder-form and bulk to Station, where belt ores and ice
became structure, decks, machine parts and solar cells, fuel and oxygen. *Lindy* would haul only between belt and oreship, taking the rich-
est small bits in her sling, tagging any larger finds for abler ships on a
one-tenth split. She even had an advantage in her size: she could go

gnatlike into stretches of the belt no larger ship would risk and, supplied by those larger ships, attach limpets to boost a worthwhile prize within reach: *that* kind of risk was negotiable.

And if she broke down in Endeavor's belt and killed her crew, well, that was the chance the Murray-Gaineses took, like all the rest who gambled on a future at Endeavor, on the hope of piling up credits in the station's bank faster than they needed to consume them, credits and stock which would increase in worth as the station grew, which was how marginal operators like the Murray-Gaineses hoped to get a lease on a safer ship and link into some forming Endeavor combine.

There was Endeavor Station: that was the first step. *Rightwise* let go the clamps; the Murray-Gaineses sweated through the unpowered docking and the checkout, enjoyed one modest round of drinks at the cheapest of Endeavor Station's four cheap bars, and opened their station account in Endeavor's cubbyhole of a docking office, red-eyed and exhausted and anxious to pay off *Rightwise* and get *Lindy* clear and away before they accumulated any additional dock charge.

So they applied for their papers and local number, paid their freight and registered their ship forthwith with hardly more formality than a clerical stamp, because *Lindy* was so ridiculously small there was no question of illicit weaponry or criminal record. She became *STAR-STATION ENDEAVOR INSYSTEM SHIP 243 Lindy,* attached to SSEIS 1, the oreship/smelter *Ajax.* She had a home.

And the Murrays and Paul Gaines, free and clear of debt, went off arm in arm to *Lindy*'s obscure berth just under the maindawn limit which would have logged them a second day's dock charge. They boarded and settled into that cramped interior, ran their checks of the charging that the station had done in their absence, and put her out under her own power without further ado, headed for Endeavor's belt.

For a little while they had an aftward single G, in the acceleration which boosted them to their passage velocity; but after that small push they went inertial and null, in which condition they would live and work three to six months at a stretch.

They had bought three bottles of Downer wine for their stores. Those were for their first tour's completion. They expected success. They were high on the anticipation of it. Rafe Murray, his sister Jillan, merchanter brats; Paul Gaines, of Fargone's deep-miners, unlikely friendship, war-flotsam that they were. But there was no doubt in them, no division, when playmates had grown up and married: and Rafe was well content. "It's tight quarters," Jillan had said to her brother when they talked about Endeavor and their partnership. "It's a long time out there, Rafe; it's going to be real long; and real lonely."

Paul Gaines had said much the same, in the way Paul could, because he and Rafe were close as brothers. "So, well," Rafe had answered, "I'll turn my back."

They called Rafe, half-joking, half-not, their Old Man, at twenty-two. That meant captain, on a larger ship. And they *were* his. Jillan planned on children in a merchanter-woman's way. They were life, and she could get them, with any man; but, unmerchanter-like, she married Paul, for good, for permanent, not to lose him, and snared him in their dream. Their children would be Murrays; would grow up to the Name that the War had robbed of a ship and almost killed out entire . . . and he dreamed with desperate fervor, did Rafe Murray, of holding Murray offspring in his arms, of a ship filled with youngsters—being himself a merchanter-man and incapable of pregnancy, which was how, after all, children got on ships: merchanter-women made them, and merchanter-women got his and took them to other ships which did not need them half so desperately.

He had had his partnerings with the women of *Rightwise* and bade all that good-bye—"Go sleepover," Paul had advised him on Endeavor dock. "Do you good."

"Money," he had said, meaning they could not spare the cost of a room, or the time. "Had my time on *Rightwise.* That's enough. I'm tired."

Paul had just looked at him, with pity in his eyes.

"What do you want?" he had answered then. "Had it last night. Three *Rightwisers.* Wore me out." And Jillan walked up just then, so there was no more argument.

"We'll have a ship," Rafe had sworn to Jillan once, when they were nine and eight, and their mother and their uncle died, last of old freighter *Lindy*'s crew, both at once, in Fargone's belt. Getting to deep space again had been *their* dream; it was all the legacy they left, except a pair of silver crew-pins and a Name without a ship.

So Rafe held Jillan by him—*Don't leave me, don't go stationer on me. You take your men; give me kids—give me that, and I'll give you—all I've got, all I'll ever have.*

Don't you leave me, Jillan had said back, equally dogged. *You be the Old Man, that's what you'll be. Don't you leave me and go forget your name. Don't you do that, ever.* And she worked with him and sweated and lived poor to bank every credit that came their way.

Most, she got him Paul Gaines, lured a miner-orphan to work with them, to risk his neck, to throw his money into it, Paul's station-share, every credit they three could gain by work from scrubbing deck to serving hire-on crew to miners when they could get a berth.

Having children waited. Waited for the ship.

And Endeavor and a dilapidated pusher-ship were the purchase of all they had.

Rafe took first watch. He caught a reflection on the leftmost screen of Jillan and Paul in their sleeping web behind his chair, fallen asleep despite their attempt to keep him company, singing and joking. They had been quite a handful of minutes and there they drifted, collapsed together, like times the three of them had hidden to sleep, three kids on Fargone, making a ship out of a shipping canister, all tucked up in the dark and secret inside, dreaming they were exploring and that stars and infinity surrounded their little shell.

$$\boxed{3/23/55}$$

Mass.

< > came fully alert, feeling that certain tug at < >'s substance which meant something large disturbing the continuum.

Trishanamarandu-kepta could have overjumped the hazard, of course, adjusting course in mid-jump with the facility of vast power and a sentience which treated the mindcrippling between of jumps like some strange ocean which < > swam with native skill. But curiosity was the rule of < >'s existence. < > skipped *down,* if such a term had relevance, an insouciant hairbreadth from disaster.

It was a bit of debris, a lump of congealed material which to the questing eye of *Trishanamarandu-kepta* appeared as a blackness, a disruption, a point of great mass.

It was a failed star, an overambitious planet, a wanderer in the wide dark which had given up almost all its heat to the void and meant nothing any longer but a pockmark in spacetime.

It was a bit of the history of this region, telling < > something of the formational past. It was nothing remarkable in itself. The remarkable time for it had long since passed, the violent death of some far greater star hereabouts. *That* would have been a sight.

< > journeyed, pursuing that thread of thought with some pleasure, charted the point of mass in < >'s indelible memory in the process.

The inevitable babble of curiosity had begun among the passengers. < >'s wakings were of interest to them. < > answered them curtly and leaped out into the deep again, heading simply to the next star, as < > did, having both eternity *and* jump capacity at < >'s disposal.

There was no hurry. There was nowhere in particular to go; and everywhere, of course. < > was now awake, lazily considering galactic motion and the likely center of that ancient supernova.

Such star-deaths begat descendants.

Chapter Two

10/2/55

The Downer wine was opened, nullstopped and passed hand to hand in celebration. Music poured from *Lindy*'s com-system. There was food in the freezer, water in the tanks, and a start to the fortunes of the Murray-Gaineses, a respectable number of credits logged on the orehauler *Ajax,* from what they had delivered and a share of what others had brought in with their beeper tags. They were bathed, shaved and fresh-scented from a docking and sleepover on *Ajax.* Even *Lindy* herself had a mint-new antiseptic tang to her air from the purging she had gotten during the hours of her stay.

"None of them," Jillan said, drifting free, "none of them believed we could have come in filled that fast. No savvy at all, these so-named miners."

"Baths," Paul Gaines murmured, and took the wine in both hands for his turn, smug bliss on his square face when he had drunk. "We're civilized again."

"Drink to that," Rafe agreed. "Here's to the next load. How long's it going to take us?"

"Under two months," Jillan proposed. "Thirty tags and a full sling."

"We can do it." Rafe was extravagant. He felt a surge of warmth, thinking on an *Ajax* woman who had opened her cabin to him in his onship time. He was feeling at ease with everything and everyone. He gave a quirk of a smile at Jillan and Paul, whose privacy was one of the storage pods when they were down on supplies, but they were full stocked now, with solid credit to their account, stock bought in Endeavor itself. "Someday," he said, "when we're very old we can tell this to our kids and they won't believe it."

"Drink to someday," Paul said, hugging Jillan with one arm, the bottle in the other. The motion started a drift and spin. Rafe snagged the bottle from Paul's hand as they passed, laughing at them as the hug became a tumble, the two of them lost in each other and not needing that bottle in the least.

I love them, Rafe thought with an unaccustomed pang, with tears in his eyes he had no shame for. His sister and his best friend. His whole life was neatly knitted up together; and maybe next year they could build old *Lindy* a little larger. Jillan could look to family-getting then, lie up on *Ajax* for the first baby; be with them thereafter—close quarters, but merchanter youngsters learned touch and not-touch, scramble and take-hold before they were steady on their feet.

And even for himself—for his own comfort—Endeavor was a haven for the orphaned, the displaced of the War, people like themselves, taking a last-ditch chance. There might be some woman someday, somehow, willing to take the kind of risk they posed.

Someone rare, like Paul.

"Drink up," Jillan insisted, drifting down with Paul. The embrace opened . . . a little frown had crossed Jillan's face at the sight of his; and Paul's expression mirrored the same concern. For that, for a thousand, thousand things, he loved them.

He grinned, and drank, and sent their bottle their way.

$$\boxed{10/9/55}$$

Trishanamarandu-kepta was in pursuit of delicate reckonings, had chased plottings round and round and busily gathered data in observation of the region. < > might have missed the ship entirely otherwise.

< > detected it in the Between, a meeting of which the ship might or might not be aware. It was small and slow, a bare ripple of presence.

It too was a consequence of that ancient star-death . . . or came here because of it. Weak as it seemed, it might well use mass like that which < > had recently visited as an anchor, a navigation fix when the distance between stars was too great for it. < > diverted < >'s self from < >'s previous heading and followed the ship, eager and intent, coming *down* at another such pockmark in the continuum, where < >'s small quarry had surfaced and paused.

(!), < > sent at once, in pulses along the whole range of < >'s transmitters. *(!!!) (!!!!!)* It was an ancient pattern, useful where there was no possibility of linguistic similarity and no reasonable guarantee of a similar range of perceptions. < > waited for response on any wavelength.

Waited.

Waited.

Even delays in response were informational. This might be recovery time, for senses severely disorganized by jumpspace. Some species were particularly affected by the experience. It might be slow consideration of the pulse message. The length of time to decide on reply, the manner of answer, whether echo or addition, whether linear or pyramidal . . . species varied in their apprehension of the question.

The small ship remained some time at residual velocity, though headed toward the hazard of the dark mass by which it steered. Presumably it was aware of the danger of its course.

< > remained wary, having seen many variations on such meetings, some proceeding to sudden attack; some to approach; some to headlong flight; some even to suicide, which might be what was in progress as a result of that unchecked velocity.

Or possibly, remotely, the ship had suffered some malfunction. < > retained corresponding velocity and kept the same interval, confident in < >'s own agility and wondering whether the ship under observation could still escape.

< > observed, which was < >'s only present interest.

The little ship suddenly flicked out again into jump. < > followed, ignoring the babble from the passengers, which had been building and now broke into chaos.

Quiet, < > wished them all, afire with the passion of a new interest in existence.

The pursuit came *down* again as < > had hoped, at a star teeming with activity on a broad range of wavelengths.

Life.

A whole spacefaring civilization.

It was like rain after ages-long drought; repletion after famine. < > stretched, enlivened capacities dormant for centuries, power like a great silent shout going through < >'s body.

Withdraw, some of the passengers wished < >. *You'll get us all killed.*

There was humor in that. < > laughed. < > could, after < >'s fashion.

Attack, others raved, that being their natures.

Hush, < > said. *Just watch.*

We trusted you, <₋> mourned.

< > ignored all the voices and stayed on course.

1/12/56

The intruder and its quarry went unnoticed for a time in Endeavor Station Central. Boards still showed clear. The trouble at the instant of its arrival was still a long, lightbound way out.

Ships closer to that arrival point picked up the situation and started relaying the signal as they moved in panic.

Three hours after arrival, Central longscan picked up a blip just above the ecliptic and beeped, routinely calling a human operator's attention to that seldom active screen, which might register an arrival once or twice a month.

But not headed into central system plane, where no incoming ship belonged, vectored at jumpship velocities toward the precise area of the belt that was worked by Endeavor miners. Comp plotted a colored fan of possible courses, and someone swore, with feeling.

A second beep an instant later froze the several techs in their seats; and *"Lord!"* a scan tech breathed, because that second blip was *close* to the first one.

"Check your pickup," the supervisor said, walking near that station in the general murmur of dismay.

That had nearly been collision out there three lightbound hours ago. The odds against two unscheduled merchanters coinciding in Endeavor's vast untrafficked space, illegally in system plane, were out of all reason.

"Tandem jump?" the tech wondered, pushing buttons to reset. Tandem jumping was a military maneuver. It required hairbreadth accuracy. No merchanter risked it as routine.

"Pirate," a second tech surmised, which they were all thinking by now. There were still war troubles left, from the bad days. "Mazianni, maybe."

The supervisor hesitated from one foot to the other, wiped his face. The stationmaster was offshift, asleep. It was hours into maindark. The supervisor was alterday chief, second highest on the station. The red-alert button was in front of him on the board, unused for all of Endeavor's existence.

". . . it's *behind* us," he heard next, the merchanter frequency, from out in the range. "Endeavor Station, do you read, do you read? This is merchanter *John Liles* out of Viking. We've met a bogey out there . . . it's dragged us off mark . . . Met . . ."

Another signal was incoming. *(!) (!!!) (!!!!!)*

". . . out there at Charlie Point," the transmission from *John Liles* went on. An echo had started, *John Liles'* message relayed ship to ship from every prospector and orehauler in the system. Everyone's ears were pricked. *Bogey* was a nightmare word, a bad joke, a thing which happened to jumpspace pilots who were due for a long, long rest. But there *were* two images on scan, and a signal was incoming which made no sense. At that moment Endeavor Station seemed twice as far from the rest of mankind and twice as lonely as before.

". . . It signaled us out there and we jumped on with no proper trank. Got sick kids aboard, people shaken up. We're afraid to dump velocity; we may need what we've got. Station, get us help out here. It keeps signaling us. It's solid. We got a vid image and it's not one of ours, do you copy? *Not one of ours or anybody's.* What are we supposed to *do,* Endeavor Station?"

Everywhere that message had reached, all along the time sequence of that incoming message, ships reacted, shorthaulers and orehaulers and prospectors changing course, exchanging a babble of intership communication as they aimed for eventual refuge out of the line of events. What interval incoming jumpships could cross in mere seconds, the insystem haulers plotted in days and weeks and months: they had no hope in speed, but in their turn-tail signal of noncombatancy.

In station central, the supervisor roused out the stationmaster by intercom. The thready voice from *John Liles* went on and on, the speaker having tried to jam all the information he could into all the time he had, a little under three hours ago. Longscan techs in Endeavor Central were taking the hours-old course of the incoming vessels and making projections on the master screen, lines colored by degree of probability, along with reckonings of present position and courses of all the ships and objects everywhere in the system. Longscan was supposed to work because human logic and human body/human stress capacities were calculable, given original position, velocity, situation, ship class, and heading.

But one of those ships out there was another matter.

And *John Liles* was not dumping velocity, was hurtling in toward the station on the tightest possible bend, the exact tightness of which had to do with how that ship was rigged inside, and what its capacity, load, and capabilities were. Computers were hunting such details frantically as longscan demanded data. The projections were cone-shaped flares of color, as yet unrefined. Com was ordering some small prospectors to head their ships nadir at once because they lay within those cones.

But those longscan projections suddenly revised themselves into a second hindcast, that those miners had started moving nadir on their own initiative the moment they picked up *John Liles'* distress call the better part of three hours ago. Data began to confirm that hypothesis, communication coming in from *SSEIS 1 Ajax,* which was now a fraction nadir of original projection.

Lindy had run early in those three hours, such as *Lindy* could . . . dumped the sling and spent all she had, trying to gather velocity. Rafe plotted frantically, trying to hold a line which used the inertia they had and still would not take them into the collision hazard of the deep belt if they had to overspend. Jillan ran counterchecks on the figures and Paul was set at com, keeping a steady flow of *John Liles'* transmission.

If *Lindy* overspent and had nothing left for braking, if they survived the belt, there were three ships which might match them and snag them down before they passed out of the system and died adrift . . . if they did not hit a rock their weak directionals could not avoid . . . if the station itself survived what was coming in at them. They could all die here. Everyone. There were two military ships at Endeavor Station and *Lindy* had no hope of help from them: the military's priority in this situation was not to come after some minuscule dying miner, but to run, warning other stars—so Paul said, who had served in Fargone militia, and they had no doubt of it. It was a question of priorities, and *Lindy* was no one's priority but their own.

"How are we doing?" Rafe asked his sister, who had her eyes on other readouts. The curves were all but touching on the comp screen, one promising them collision and one offering escape.

"Got a chance," Jillan said, "if that merchanter gives us just a hair."

Paul was transmitting, calmly, advising *John Liles* they were in its path. On the E-channel, *Lindy*'s autowarning screamed collision alert: the wave of that message should have reached *John Liles* by now.

"Rafe," Jillan said, "recommend you take all the margin. Now."

"Right." Rafe asked no questions, having too much input from the boards to do anything but take it as he was told. He squeezed out the last safety margin they had before overspending, shut down on the mark, watching the computer replot the curves. In one ear, Paul was quietly, rationally advising *John Liles* that they were ten minutes from impact; in the other ear came the com flow from *John Liles* itself, babble which still pleaded with station, wanting help, advising station that they were innocent of provocation toward the bogey. "Instruction," *John Liles* begged again and again, ignoring communications from others. It was a tape playing. Possibly their medical emergency or their attention to the bogey behind them took all their wits.

"Come *on,*" Rafe muttered, flashing their docking floods in the distress code, into the diminishing interval of their light-speed message impacting the 3/4 C time-frame of *John Liles'* Doppler receivers. He was not panicked. They were all too busy for panic. The calculations flashed tighter and tighter.

"We've got to destruct," Paul said at last in a thin, strained voice. "Three of us—a thousand on that ship—O God, we've got to do it—"

Sudden static disrupted all their scan and com, blinding them. *"She's dumping,"* Jillan yelled. *John Liles* had cycled in the generation vanes, shedding velocity in pulses. They were getting the wash, like a storm passing, with a flaring of every alarm in the ship. It dissipated. *"We're all right,"* Paul yelled prematurely. In the next instant scan cleared and showed them a vast shape coming dead on. Rafe froze, braced, frail human reaction against what impact was coming at them at a mind-bending 1/10 C.

It dumped speed again, another storm of blackout. Rafe moved, trembled in the wake of it, fired directionals to correct a yaw that had added itself to their motion. Scan cleared again.

"Clear that," Rafe said. "Scan's fouled." The blip showed itself larger than *Ajax,* large as infant Endeavor Station itself.

"No," Paul said. *"Rafe, that's not the merchanter."*

"Vid," Rafe said. Paul was already flicking switches. The camera swept, a blur of stars onscreen. It targeted, swung back, locked.

The ship in view was like nothing human-built, a disc cradled in a frame warted with bubbles of no sensible geometry, in massive extrusions on frame and disc like some bizarre cratering from within. The generation vanes, if that was what those projections were, stretched about it in a tangle of webbing as if some mad spider had been at work, veiling that toadish lump in gossamer. Lightnings flickered multicolor in the webs and reflected off the warted body, a repeated sequence of pulses.

It had exited C and actually gone negative, so that their relative speeds were a narrowing slow drift.

"Twenty meters-second," Jillan read the difference. "Plus ten, plus five-five, plus five-seven K."

There were no maneuvering options. *Lindy* was already at the edge of her safety reserve, and a ship which could shift course and stop like that—could overhaul them with the merest twitch of an effort. Rafe flexed his fingers on the main throttle and let it go.

"Maybe it's curious," Jillan said under her breath. *"Liles* never said it fired."

"Got their signal," Paul said, and punched it in for both of them . . . *(!) (!!!) (!!!!!).*

"Echo it," Rafe said. They were still getting signal from *John Liles,* a screen now Dopplered in retreat, echoed from other ships. Station might be aware by now that something was amiss; but there was still the lagtime of reply to go. As yet there was only *Ajax* sending out her longscan and her frantic instruction to *John Liles.*

Lindy, on her own, facing Leviathan, sent out a tentative pulse.
(!) (!!!) (!!!!!)

Scan beeped, instant at their interval. "Bogey's moving," Jillan said in a still, calm voice. It was. "Cut the signal," Rafe said at once; and on inspiration: "Reverse the sequence and send."

(!!!!!), Paul sent. *(!!!) (!)*

No. Negative. Reverse. Keep away from us.

The bogey kept coming, but slower, feather-soft for something of its power, as if it drifted. "10.2 meters-second," Jillan read off. "Steady."

"It could shed us like dust if it wanted to," Paul said. "It's being careful."

"So we ride it out," Rafe said. A hand closed on his arm, Jillan's. He never took his eyes from the screens and instruments. Neither did she.

The bogey filled all their vid now, monstrous and flashing with strange lights, a sudden and rapid flare.

"It's braking," Jillan said. "4 . . 3 . . . relative stop."

"Station," Paul sent, "this is *SSEIS 243 Lindy,* with the bogey in full sight. It's looking us over. We're transmitting vid; all ships relay."

There was no chance of reply from station, a long timeline away. *"Relaying,"* a human ship broke in, someone calling dangerous attention to themselves by that sole and human comfort.

"Thank you," Paul said, and kept the vid going, still sending.

The surface of the bogey had detail now. The warts were complex and overlapping, the smallest of the extrusions as large as *Lindy* her-

self. The camera swept the intruder, finding no marking, no sign of
any identifiable structure which might be scanning them in turn.

Suddenly scan and vid broke up.

And space did.

Chapter Three

Capture.

Trishanamarandu-kepta reached for the mote with < >'s jump field.

< > left the star, dragging the captured mote along.

Rafe had time to feel it happening. He screamed—a long, outraged *"No!"*—at the utter stupidity of dying, perhaps; at everything he lost. His voice wound strangely material through the chaos of the between, entwined with the substance and the terrified voices of Jillan and Paul. He was still screaming when the jump came, the giddy insideout pulse into *here* and *when,* falling unchecked out of infinity into substance that could be harmed. He reached out, groping wildly after controls as the instruments flashed alarm. Orientation was gone. They were moving, his body persuaded him, though he felt no G. He pushed autopilot: red lights flared at him, a bloody haze of lights and blur.

Lindy's autopilot kicked in, and it was wrong . . . he felt it, the beginning of a roll, a braking insufficient for their velocity. The wobble

Lindy had always had with the directionals betrayed her now. He tried to shut it down, while G was whipping blood to his head, rupturing vessels in his nose, a coppery taste at one with the bloody lights and the screams.

Paul and Jillan.

"Jillan!"

Paul's voice.

Tumble went on and on. Instruments broke up again, and another motion complicated the spin: autopilot malfunction. They had been dragged through jump, boosted to velocity a good part of C, and *Lindy* was helpless, uninstrumented for this kind of speed. Every move the autopilot made was wrong, complicating *Lindy*'s motion.

He fought to get his hand to the board, to do something, a long red tunnel narrowing black edges between him and the lights.

Someone screamed his name. His eyes were pressing at their sockets and his brain at his skull, his gut crawling up his rib cage to press his lungs and heart and spew its contents in a choking flood that might be hemorrhage. The tunnel narrowed and the pressure acquired a rhythm in his ears. Vision went in bursts of gray and red, and mind tumbled after.

< > maneuvered carefully to secure the ship: field seized it, stabilized it from its spinning, snugged it close. Getting it inside once stable was no problem at all.

Getting inside *it* . . . was another matter altogether.

Kill it, some advised.

< / > moved to do that. < > blocked that attempt with brutal force. An extensor probe drifted along a track and reached down, punched through the hull with very precise laser bursts and bled off an atmosphere sample from the innermost cavity.

Nitrogen, argon, carbon dioxide, oxygen . . . *Trishanamarandukepta* had no internal atmosphere. < > started acquiring one, here and in other sections.

< > had no need of gravity; but < > began to acquire it, basing calculations on the diameter and rotation of the structure back at the star.

< > extended other probes and surveyed the small ship's hull, locating the major access.

The interior was, once < > had gotten a probe inside to see, messy. The occupants, stained with red fluids, stirred only feebly, and more and more extensors cooperated in freeing the occupants from their restraints, in moving them outside, while other extensors intruded into every portion of the diminutive ship, testing the instrumentation, sampling the consumables. < > flurried through incoming data in a general way, relating that and what it discovered in the tiny ship's computers, simple mathematical instruments adequate only for the most basic operations.

The subjects offered resistance, though weakly, at being containered and moved a great and rapid distance through *Trishanamarandukepta*'s twisting interior. One was very active: it thrashed about at intervals, losing strength and smearing the transparent case with red fluids at every outburst, which indicated rapidly diminishing returns, whether this motion was voluntary or not. It screamed intermittently, and whether this was communication remained to be judged.

It screamed a very long scream when it was positioned in the apparatus and the recorder came on and played through its nervous system. So did the other two. Most vocal organisms would.

Each collapsed after the initial spasm. Vital signs continued in a series of wild fluctuations which seemed to indicate profound shock. < > maintained them within the recorder-field and realigned them with the hologrammatic impression < > had taken.

< > took cell samples, fluid samples, analyzed the physical structures from the whole to the microscopic and chemical while the entities remained conscious. < > was careful, well aware that some of the procedures might cause pain. < > reduced what wild response < > could, elicited occasional murmurings from the subjects. < > recorded those sounds and played them back; played back all response it had ever gotten from this species, here and from the other ship and from the star system in general.

The subjects responded. Sympathetically, on both recorded words and answers, the holo images < > had constructed . . . reacted.

< > used lights and sounds and other stimuli, and mapped reflexes in the hologrammatic brains, obtaining sensory reactions from the imprints along the appropriate pathways. < > discovered what seemed to be a rest state and maintained the organisms close to sleep,

yet able to react and speak, prolonging this interrogation in words and sensations.

The two weakest sank deeper, refusing when prodded to come out of this state, eventually deteriorating so that it required more and more stimulus to keep them functioning. At last decomposition set in.

The third subject remained in sleep-state. $<>$ questioned it further and it reacted in dazed compliance.

The simulacra still reacted . . . all three of them.

The surviving organism fell into deeper and deeper sleep and $<>$ let it rest.

$<>$ further examined the remains of the other two, analyzed them in their failure, finally committed them to cryostorage.

$<>$ wasted nothing that $<>$ took in.

Rafe moved, and knew that he moved. He felt no pain. His limbs seemed adrift in void, and when he opened his eyes he thought that he was blind.

"Jillan!" he cried, struggling to stand, reaching out with his hands. "Paul, Jillan!"

"Rafe—!" Jillan's voice came back; and she was there, coming toward him in the starless void. Paul followed. They were naked, both; so was he; and their bodies glowed like lamps in the utter dark, as if they were their own light, and all the light there was. They began to run toward him, and he ran, caught Jillan in his arms, and Paul, ashamed for his nakedness and theirs and not caring, not caring anything but to hug their warmth against him. He felt the texture of their skin, their hands on him, their arms about him.

He wept, shamelessly. There was a great deal of tears, that first, that most important and human thing. "You're here," Jillan kept saying; "you're all right, we've got you, oh Rafe, we've got you—hold on."

—Because the fainting-feeling was on him, and they all three seemed to drift, to whirl, to travel in this dark. There were sounds, far wails, like wind. Something brushed past them through the dark, vast and impersonal, like the whisper of a draft.

"Where have we got to?" Paul wondered, and Rafe looked at Paul and looked at Jillan as they stood disengaged, in this dark nowhere.

"I don't know," he said, ashamed for his helplessness to tell them. *I'm scared.* He kept that behind his teeth. He looked about him, into nothing at all, and kept remembering jump, and the sinuous wave of arms.

"There was something—" Jillan said, her teeth chattering. "Oh God, God—" She stood there, shivering in her nakedness, and Paul hugged her against him. "Don't," he said, "don't. Don't think, don't—"

"We're through jump," Rafe said as firmly as he could, filling the void, the dark about them all with words to listen to, making them fix on him. "There was that bogey; it's got us. Remember? That's where we are. It's got us in the dark, and we can't come undone, you hear me, both of you. Let's think our way out of this. It's kept us alive and together. That's something, isn't it?"

They said nothing. Their faces were dreadful, full of shadows within their glowing flesh.

"Why no light?" Jillan asked.

"Maybe they don't have eyes," Paul said.

She looked at her glowing hands, at him, at Paul, with a whole dreadful range of surmises in that glance.

"It's some kind of effect," Rafe said, searching for any plausible thing, "some light trick. That's all."

"Sure," said Paul, attempting cheerfulness, "sure. Who knows what kind of thing." But his voice was thin. He walked a little distance away and distances themselves played tricks, so that he became small rapidly, as if he strode meters at a time. "Come back," Rafe said, and Paul turned, looking small and frightened.

"God, what is this place?"

"I'm cold," Jillan said, hugging herself; but the air was not cold at all; it was nothing. It was the nakedness that diminished all of them, that made them vulnerable, the dark that made them blind.

"Look," Rafe said, "let's not go off crazy. We can't ask questions. You have to know something to ask questions and we don't. We've got no referents. We're just alive, that's all—" *They hurt us,* his memory insisted, and he fought that down. "Nothing matters but now and facts, and facts we're short of. Calm down."

"What do we do?" Jillan asked.

"We stay close together," he said, "and we try not to lose each other. Let's try to find a wall, a door, somewhere in this place." He took her hand and walked to Paul, in those curious several-meter steps that were the law here, while Paul stared at them with nightmare in his eyes that showed dark as the dark about them. "We're having trouble with our senses," Rafe said to them both, and even his voice seemed lost in void. "Maybe it isn't even dark. Jump can do things to you. We weren't tranked."

"You mean we're crazy," Paul said. "All three of us at once. Or do I imagine you? Or you us? Or what?"

"I'm saying our eyes aren't working right."

"What about the floor?" Paul said, sinking to one knee, touching what felt like air underfoot. "I don't feel anything. I don't feel *anything!* I don't even feel my breathing. Like it isn't air."

"We'll come out of it," Jillan said, and drew Paul to his feet. "Paul, we'll make it. Rafe's right; it's the jump; it's done something to us. We're not getting sense out of it."

"Between?" Paul asked, blinking as if he had just thought of that. "You mean we're still in hyperspace? Could that be it?"

"Maybe," Rafe said, clinging to that hope.

"O God," Paul murmured, shaking his head, and looked up and about again—hopeless to ask how long, how far, where there was no reference. "That makes sense."

Then light began to grow about them, white and green. It took on shadows of shapes.

It became a nightmare, bits and pieces of *Lindy* rooted in a noded, serpentine hallway fuzzed in gossamer like spiderweb over carpet. There stood the seats, part of the control console, the EVApod standing at attention like some humanoid monster grown from the wall at an angle. A row of luminants snaked like a chain of warts down the center of the noded ceiling, giving what light there was.

And Rafe saw himself lying there naked on the floor.

"That's *you,*" Jillan moaned. "Rafe, what's happening to us?"

The lights went dim again. Rafe strode forward, desperate, recalling how the dying saw their bodies from some other vantage. He felt the cold, felt a vast love of that poor wounded flesh that was himself, wanting it back again.

"*Rafe!*" Jillan called, and the horror dawned on him, that they were dead, that Jillan and Paul were bodiless, and he almost was. "*Rafe!*"

The dark closed about him and he fought it, trying to get back to the light. He felt their hands like claws, clutching at him to drag him back to death with them.

"Let me go," he cried, "let me go!"—cursing their selfishness.

Rafe moved, and knew that he moved. He felt other things, pain, and chill, and G holding him supine against a cloth surface. He opened his eyes and kept them open, on a graygreen arched ceiling of warts and white fuzz, like what his fingers and body felt under him, soft and rough like carpet. He felt a draft on all his skin so that he knew he was naked. His heart started speeding, his mind sorting. *"Jillan—Jillan, Paul?"* He rolled over, wincing from torn muscles, from a sudden lancing pain from eyes to the back of his skull.

Dim distance, warts and cobwebby stuff snaked on and on as far as he could see, graygreen to white in an irregular corridor, lumpish and winding as if the place abhorred a straight line.

He scrambled to his knees, trembling, and stopped cold. His blurred eyes fixed on nightmare. Bits and pieces of *Lindy* were rooted in the tunnel, the seats, part of the control console, the EVApod standing there like some humanoid monster rising out of the warted, gossamer wall at an angle. The sanitary compartment stood intact, enveloped in graygreen moss and cobweb above and below. The storage cabinets thrust up from the floor like angled teeth.

He pressed his hands to his face and rubbed his eyes, felt days-old stubble on his jaw. He staggered erect, his muscles gone weak from those lost days. The corridor went on and on in that direction too, beyond the point where *Lindy*'s parts gave out, mossy and cobwebbed, all lit from luminous warts in the ceiling, irregularly placed, a line of lights winding with the serpentine turns.

"Jillan," he called aloud. "Paul?" His voice was terrible in that stillness. He turned, looked all about him, down two ways of the corridor equally desolate and strange and vanishing into turns and dark.

"Jillan," he shouted suddenly, desperate. "Jillan, Paul, do you hear me?"

Silence.

He searched for other sleepers, staggered among the nightmare remnants of *Lindy* until there were no more, and he faced only the warted corridor ahead. He went back and opened all the doors of the cabinets and the cases, even looked into the dark faceplate of the EVApod, fearing what he might find.

All empty. There were *Lindy*'s stores, food, supplies, clothing in the lockers . . . his, Paul's, Jillan's, all as it ought to be. He looked up in the panicked imagination of someone watching him. Nothing. No indication of any living soul.

He took clothes from his locker, dressed painfully, pulling seams past sore joints. He found his watch, his soft-soled boots, his tags . . . the pin that was from the old, the first *Lindy,* that had been his uncle's. He sat down on the floor and put on the boots and the rest of it. His hands shook. His heart was doubling its beats. He went through mundane motions in this insane place and tried to go on functioning while flashes of memory came back, disjointed. He remembered the surface of the alien vessel and saw the same architecture everywhere about him. He had no doubt where he was. He remembered jump-space . . . and no trank; remembered (he had thought) dying—

And worse things. Far worse than the nightmare of *Lindy*'s dissected portions at his side. Arms. Arms snaking into the ship. Machinery. Pain.

Pain.

"Jillan . . . Paul. . . ." He staggered up, hesitated between forward and back, the two ways from this place being alike. *"Who are you?"* he screamed at the ceiling.

There was no answer.

He walked the direction his mind sorted as *ahead,* treading around the hummocks of the floor. The wall evolved to white instead of graygreen; he touched it, but it felt like the other had felt . . . gossamer silk to a light touch, but rough to a harder one, like cobweb over stiff carpet, resisting compaction. The walls went on in alternate color changes, areas of graygreen, areas of white, all warted and noded and twisting and cobwebbed, and he tried to think what manner of inhabitant might call this home.

They were across jump: that memory was solid. Other recollections came, of confinement like a coffin; of pain running through all his nerves at once, of pain so intense it was sight and hearing and being burned alive and clawed apart from inside; of pain that still ached through joints and bone and made his muscles shake. All the voices of the other ships had rung in his skull at once, over and over; Jillan's voice and Paul's voice and the voice of *John Liles* all wound together, pleading for help and rescue.

They had been in this place with him. He remembered them screaming, amid the pain. Remembered Paul's voice calling his name.

There was no knowing where they had been brought, how far, how long. The intruder had simply dragged them off in its field, off into the dark, as if Endeavor star had been the firelight and this beast had just bounded into the light to snatch a victim . . . to take it where it could do what it liked, at its leisure. There was no hope of help. They could be taken apart piece by piece and the whole procedure transmitted to Endeavor on vid, and there was nothing Endeavor could do about it. There was nothing here, not even human sympathy.

"Jillan," he called from time to time. It grew harder and harder to challenge that silence, which was greater and deeper than any he had known in his stationbound, shipbound life. He felt a pulse somewhere too deep for proper hearing, the working of some constant machinery . . . but no sound of fans, no ping of heating and cooling or sound of hydraulics. No feeling of being on a ship under acceleration. Just more and more corridor, cobwebbed, warted silence.

His knees grew weak in walking. He thought that it might be shock catching up to him. He realized he had no idea where he was going or why, and that his walking itself was reasonless. He sat down to rest and dropped his head into his arms.

The lights went out.

He sprang up in alarm, facing what light remained, far down the corridor. He went for the lighted section, stumbling over the nodes, hurrying until his ribs hurt—and those lights went out as he reached them as lights further on flared into life.

He understood the game then, that he was watched, that it/they wanted him to come—to them, to something. He moved helplessly toward the light that beckoned, afraid of dark and blindness in this place. They threatened to shut him off from his primary sense and he reacted in animal instinct, knowing what they were doing to him and how simply; and hoping somewhere at gut level that doing what they wanted might bring him to where Jillan and Paul were. He ran, even hurting, slowed only as his strength gave out and he fell farther and farther behind the lights until they stayed on at the limit of his sight, in one fixed sector, beyond which was unremedied dark. He reached that place as the lights dimmed and moved on into vastness where the walls were walls and were farther and farther apart.

Sweat chilled his face. What had been a limp became a stagger. He tended more and more toward the right-hand wall as the left-hand one strayed off into black, as the whole corridor opened into the likeness of a vast cavern, one with low knobbed points to the ceiling like a cavern of warts, whose farther reaches were wrapped in deepening shadow.

A sudden bright light speared from the ceiling in front of him. He flung an arm across his eyes. "Who are you?" he asked the light and the darkness, irrational as cursing: there had been no answers and he expected none.

"I don't know," a voice came back to him, and *he* was standing there, a naked man at one heartbeat strange and then—like recognizing a mirror where one had expected none—altogether familiar. He was staring at himself, at what might have been a mirror in its expression of shock and fear—he knew that look, was startled when it lifted a hand he had not lifted and opposed itself to him.

"Damn you," he cried to the invisible, the manipulator. *"Damn you,* use your own shape!"

"I am," the doppelganger said. Tears glistened in his/its eyes. "O God, don't—don't look like that. Help me. I don't know where I am."

"Liar," he told himself.

"Rafe." The voice drifted from the lips, his own, uncertain and lost and vague. "Please. Listen to me. You're awake. I'm you. I think I am. I don't know. Please—" The doppelganger walked, sat down above a node, not quite phasing with it. It tucked its bare knees up, locked its arms about them, looked up at him with eyes full of shadow, as if the image were breaking down. "Please sit and talk with me."

He watched his own face shape words. The lips trembled, quirks in the chin that he knew and felt in his own gut, as if it were himself fighting tears, fighting for his dignity. It hurt to watch. He was trembling as if the tears were his, and they began to be. "Where's Jillan? Where's Paul? Can you tell me that?"

"Sit down. Please, sit down."

He found a place and sat, hugged his knees up until he realized he had taken the mirror pose, clothed version and naked one. His gut heaved, and he swallowed hard. "What's your name?" he asked.

"Rafe. You have to call me something. I'm you. Or something like. I can see you—there. I guess you can see me. Do I look like you?"

"Where's Jillan and Paul? The people with me—where are they?"

"They're—" The doppelganger pointed off toward the dark outside the light. "They're somewhere about. Not speaking to me. Please—let me try to explain this. I don't know where their bodies are. I found you. Me. Lying there. I thought—you know, the way you can see yourself—they say you can see yourself when you die. You float up near the ceiling and look down and see yourself lying there, and you can hear, and you don't want to go back—But I wanted to. I tried. Jillan and Paul—they're like me. They're with me. I think they are."

"You're talking nonsense." He hugged himself, trying not to shiver, but the thought kept circling him that it was not an alien in front of him. He wanted it to be. He wanted it to change into something else, anything else. "Evaporate, why don't you?"

"Please." The doppelganger seemed to shiver. Tears ran down its face. "I think I might. I don't know. Maybe I'm you, a part of you, and we got separated somehow."

"Maybe I'm dreaming this."

"Or I am. But I don't think so. There's this dark place. I come and go out of it and I don't know how. You walk and you cover so much ground you can get lost. Maybe you can lose yourself and not get back. I'm afraid that's what's happened to Jillan and Paul. I think they're off looking—looking for their own selves. Like you. They're not taking this well. I'm scared. Please don't look like that."

"God, what do you expect me to look like?"

"I know. I know. I feel it like we were still connected when you look like that."

"You read my mind. Is that it? You're the alien. You just pick up on what I think, what I'd think—"

"Don't." The doppelganger shook its head, wiped a fist across its mouth in an expression which was his own. "Don't do that. I know I'm not. I know. I wouldn't choose to feel like this if I had a choice. I don't remember being anything else. I was born at Fargone; Jillan's my sister; our kin all died—"

"Cut it!"

"It's all I know. It's all I know, and—Rafe—I remember the jump, remember this place we were in—"

He remembered too, the terror, the waving arms, the pain, the ungodly pain. . . .

"I woke up in the dark," the doppelganger said. "And they were with me, Jillan was, and Paul. And somehow I found you. You were lying on the floor. I tried to get to you. I thought—I thought we were dying then. That I had to get back."

"I don't know why I'm talking to you." Rafe put his head down, ran his hand through his hair, looked up again in the earnest hope the apparition would have gone. It had not. It stared at him, a mirror image of despair.

"I'm afraid," it said. "O God, I'm scared."

"Where are they?"

"I don't know."

He drew a deep breath and got to his feet, came closer and saw the image lose its coherency at close range. "I can see through you."

"Can you?"

"You're an image. That's all you are." He kept walking till the image lost all its coherency and he moved into it. He saw it projected around his outstretched hand. "Fake!"

"But I'm here," the voice persisted, forlorn, with an edge of panic. "Don't. Don't do that. Back off. Please back off."

He swept his arm about as if that could scatter it, like vapor. "You're *nothing*, hear?"

There was no answer. The image reconstituted itself a little way away, naked and frightened looking. Tears still glistened on its face.

"I think," it said, "I think—somehow they made me. I don't know how. While you were asleep. O God, hold onto me. Please hold onto me."

"How?" The terror in the voice was real. It hurt him, so that at once he wanted to deal it hurt and heal it. "I can't touch you. You're not *here*, do you hear me? Wherever you are, it's not here."

"I think—think they made me out of you. Up to—I don't know how long ago—we have the same memories, because I was you." The doppelganger folded his hands over his nakedness, wistful, lost-looking, in a dreadful calm. "I'm really scared. But I guess I haven't got title to be. All I am—I guess—is you."

"Look—" he said to himself, hurting for himself, feeling half mad. "Look. Where are you? Can you tell that?"

"Here. Just here. There's that other place. But it's only dark. I don't want to go back there."

"I think—I think they've made some kind of android."

"I might be."

"The Jillan and Paul with you—they're like you?"

"I don't know."

"What do you mean you don't know? Bring them here."

"I don't know how to look."

"Liar." He flung his arm at the doppelganger, somewhere between hate and pity. "Go try."

"It's dark out there."

He wanted to laugh, to curse, to weep. He did none of them, feeling a shaking in his knees, a mounting terror. He had never liked dark confined spaces. Crawlways, like Fargone mines. "Go on," he said. "Come back when you know something."

And that too was mad.

"Will you—" his double asked, in a faint thin voice, "will you find something to call me—so I have a name?"

"Name yourself."

"*You* name me," the other said, and sent chills up his spine.

"Rafe," Rafe said. He could not commit that ultimate robbery. "That's what you are, isn't it?"

The shoulders straightened, the head came up, touching a chord in him, as if he had discovered courage in himself he had never seen. "That's what I am," the doppelganger said. "Brother."

And it walked away.

What it had said chilled him, that it had said a thing he had not dreamed to say.

He sat down where he was, locked his arms over his head, thinking that he might have witnesses.

He looked up when he had got his breath back.

"If you've built that thing," he said to the walls, able to think of it as *thing* when he was not staring at it face to face, "you've got some way to interpret it. Haven't you? You understand? Why are you doing this?"

There was no answer. He sat there until the strength had returned to his legs and then he began carefully to retrace his way back to the small horror that was his, the place stocked with food that he could use.

Habitat, he thought. *As if I were an animal.* He nursed hope, all the same, that if he had come through it, if the pain was done, then their captors were only being careful. It did not guarantee that they were benign. There were darknesses in his mind that refused to come into the light, the memory of the ship that had done what no ship ought to do; of pain—but they might have been ignorant, or in a hurry to save them.

So he built up his hope. The lights came on ahead of him, at an easy pace. He went, looking over his shoulder from time to time, and quickly forward, fearing ambushes.

He remembered the bogey's size, like the starstation itself. Hurling that into jump took more power than any engine had a right to use; and for the rest, for technology that could tear a mind apart and reconstitute it inside an android—that was the stuff of suppositions and what-ifs, spacers' yarns and books. No one did such things.

No one jumped a station-sized mass. By the laws he knew, nothing could, that did not conform to the conditions of a black hole. And it did it from virtual standstill.

He did not run when he had home in sight; he restrained himself, but his knees were shaking.

He sat down when he had gotten there, in the chair before the disjointed console, in the insane debris of *Lindy*'s corpse, and bowed his head onto his arms, because it ached.

Ached as if something were rent away from him.

He wiped his eyes and idly flipped a switch, jumped when a screen flared to life and gave him star-view.

He tried the controls, and there was nothing.

Com, he thought, and spun the chair about, flipping switches, opening a channel, hoping it went somewhere. "Hello," he said to it, to whatever was listening. "Hello—hello."

"Aaaiiiiiiiiiiieeeeeeee!"

"Damn!" he yelled back at it, reaction; and trembled after he had cut it off.

He went on, shaking, trying not to think at all, putting himself through insane routine of instrument checkout, as if he were still on *Lindy*'s bridge and not managing her pieces in this madness.

Com was connected to something—what, he had no wish to know. Vid gave him starfield, but he had no referent. The computer still worked, at least in areas the board had not lost. The lights still worked; one of the fans did, insanely; their tapes were still there, but the music would break his heart.

He slumped over finally and hid the sight of it from his eyes, suspecting worse ahead. It played games with him. He already knew that they were cruel.

Chapter Four

There was the dark, forever the void, and Rafe moved in it, calling sometimes—"Jillan, Paul—" but no one answered.

He should have been cold, he thought; but he had no more sense of the air about him than he had of the floor underfoot.

He turned in different directions, in which he found himself making slower and slower progress, as if he walked against a wind and then found himself facing (he thought) entirely a different direction than before.

"Aaaiiiiiiiiii!" something howled at him, went rushing past with a glow and a wail like nothing he had ever heard, and he scrambled back, braced for an attack.

It went away, just sped off insanely howling into the dark, and he sank down and crouched there in his nakedness, protecting himself in the only way he had, which was simply to hug his knees close and sit and tremble, totally blind except for the view of his own limbs.

"Jillan," he whispered to the void, terrified of making any noise, any sound that would bring the howler back. His own gold-glowing flesh seemed all too conspicuous, beacon to any predator.

Android. He reminded himself what he was, that he could not be harmed; but his memories insisted he was Rafe Murray. It was all he knew how to be. And he knew now that they were not alone in this dark place.

At last he got himself to his feet and moved again, no longer sure in what direction he had been going, no longer sure but what the darkness concealed traps ahead, or that he was not being stalked behind.

"Jillan," he called aloud. "Paul."

Had that been one of the aliens—that passing, mindless wail, or some other victim fleeing God-knew-what ahead?

What is *this place?*

They were androids. That was what they were, what he had been when he had met his living body—met Rafe. Something had projected him into that green-noded corridor.

But then, he reasoned, Rafe ought to have been a projection sent in turn to him, and he had not been. Viewpoint troubled him, how he had seen through hologrammatic eyes. How that Rafe had thrust his hand into the heart of him and cursed him—*Evaporate, why don't you?*

Why not? a small voice said. *If I'm an android they can make me what they like. Can't they?*

Maybe they have.

Fake, that other Rafe had said, screaming at him his outrage at self-robbery.

That Rafe Murray had the scars, the bruises, the pain that proved his title to flesh and life.

Where are we? Where are Jillan and Paul? What will they do to us? What have they done already and what am I?

"Jillan," he screamed with all his force. "Paul! Answer me! *Answer me . . .*" with the terror that he would never find them, that they had been taken away to some final disposition, and that it would take him soon, questions all unanswered.

Why did they make us?

He feared truths, that whoever had made him could throw some switch and bring him somewhere else, back where they had made him, back to that place with the machinery and the blood; perhaps would unmake him then. He feared death—that it was still possible for him.

"Aaaaaaaaaaaauuuuu!" Another thing passed him, roaring like some machine out of control, and he stopped, stood trembling until it had faded into the distance.

"Stop playing games with me," he said quietly, trusting of a sudden that something heard him better than it would hear that other, living Rafe. *"Do you hear me? I'm not impressed."*

Could it speak any human tongue? Had it learned, was it learning now?

"Damn you," he said conversationally, shrugged and kept walking, pretending indifference inside and out. But the cold that was not truly in the air had lodged beneath the heart. *God,* he appealed to the invisible—he was Catholic, at least the Murrays had always been; but God —God was for something that had the attributes of life.

Rafe One had God; he had Them. It. Whatever had made him. It might flip a switch, speak a word, reach into him and turn him inside out for a joke. That was power enough.

"Jillan!" he yelled, angry—He could still feel rage, proving—proving what? he wondered. The contradictions multiplied into howling panic. *"Jillan!"*

"Rafe?"

He turned, no more anywhere than before, in the all-encompassing dark. He saw a light coming to him, that wafted as if a wind blew it. It was Paul, and Jillan came running in his wake.

"Rafe," Jillan cried, and met him and hugged him, warm, naked flesh that reminded him flesh existed here—*synthetic?* he remembered. Paul hugged him too; and his mind went hurtling back to that howling thing in the dark, remembering that here it would be palpable and true. He shivered in their arms.

"There are *things* in here," Jillan said.

"I know, I know. I heard them," he said, holding her, being held, until the shivers went away.

"Don't go off from us again," Paul said. "Dammit, Rafe, we could get lost in here."

He broke into laughter, sobbed instead. He touched Jillan's earnest, offended face and saw her fear. "Did you find what you were looking for?"

"Dark," Jillan said. "Just dark. No way out."

"I met someone," he said to them, and let the words sink in, watching their faces as the sense of it got through. "I *met* someone."

"Who?" Jillan asked, carefully, ever so carefully, as if she feared his mind had gone.

"Myself. The body that we saw. There in the corridor. He wants to talk to you."

"You mean you went back," said Paul.

"I talked to him."

"Him?"

"Myself. He's alive, you understand that? I met him—face to face. Jillan—" he said, for she began to turn to Paul. "Jillan—we're not—not the real ones. They've made us. The memories, our bodies—We're not real."

There was devastated silence.

"If we could get back," said Paul.

"It's not a question of getting back," Rafe said, catching at Paul's arm. *"Paul, we're constructs."*

"You're out of your mind."

Rafe laughed, a sickly, sorrowful mirth. "Yes," he said. "Out of his. The way you came out of Paul's; and Jillan's out of her. Constructs, hear? Androids. Robots. Our senses—aren't reliable. We got only what the ones who made us want. God knows where we really are."

"Stop it!" Jillan cried, shaking at his arms. "Rafe, stop it, you hear me?"

He seized her and hugged her close, felt her trembling—Could an android grieve? But it was Jillan's grief, Jillan's terror. His sister's. Paul's. It was unbearable, this pain; and like the other it did not look to stop.

"Rafe," Paul said, and pulling him away into his arms, pressed his head against his shoulder and tried to soothe him as if he had gone stark mad. There was the smell of their flesh, cool and human in this sterility; the touch of their hands; the texture of their hair—Real, his senses told him. Someone was playing with their minds; that was the answer. *That's why Rafe's solid to me and I'm not that way to him.*

"Please," he said, pushing away from them. "Come with me. Let me take you to him. Talk with him."

"We've got to get out of here." Jillan's eyes had all space and void in their depths. "Rafe, pull yourself together. Don't go off like this.

They're tricks. They're all just tricks. They're working on our minds, that's what's happening. That's why none of this makes sense."

"Get out of it, how, Jillan? We came through jump. *Lindy*'s in pieces, back there in that hall."

"It's illusion. They want us to think it is. They're lying, you understand?"

"Jump wasn't a lie."

"We've got to do something to get out of here."

"Jillan—" He wanted to believe her. He wanted it with all his mind. But he suspected a dreadful thing, staring into her eyes. He suspected a whole spectrum of dreadful truths, and did not know how to tell her. "Jillan," he said as gently as he could. "Jillan, he wants to talk to you and Paul, he wants it very much."

"There is no *he!*" Paul shouted.

"Then come with me and prove it."

"There's no proving it. There's no proving anything about an illusion, except you put your hand into it and it isn't there."

"He did that to me. Put his hand through me. I wasn't there."

"You're talking crazy," Paul said.

"All you have to do is come with me. Talk to him."

"It's one of them. That's what it is."

"Maybe it is," Rafe said. He felt cold, as if a wind had blown over his soul. "But prove it to me. I'll do anything you want if you can prove it to me. Come and make me believe it. I want to believe you're right."

"Rafe," Jillan said.

"Come with me," he said, and when they seemed disposed to refuse: "Where else can we find anything out for sure?"

"All right," Jillan said, though Paul muttered otherwise. "All right. I'm coming. Come on, Paul."

She took his hand. Paul came up on his other side. He turned back the way he had come, as near he could remember, walking with two-meter strides, not knowing even if he could find that place again. But the moment he started to move it began to be about him again, the light, the noded, green-gossamer corridor, *Lindy*'s wreckage like flotsam on a reef.

And the other Rafe, the living one, sat on the floor against the wall.

That Rafe looked up in startlement and scrambled stiffly to his feet, wincing with the pain.

"Rafe," Rafe said, for it had been a long and lonely time, how long he did not know, only he had had time to meddle uselessly with the console, to shave and wash, and sleep. And now the doppelganger was back, in the shadows where his image showed best, naked as before.

And on either side of him arrived Jillan and Paul, naked, pitiful in their fear.

At least their images—whose eyes rested on him in horror, and warned him by that of their fragility. He could not hurt them. His own doppelganger—that was himself, but Jillan and Paul drove a wedge into his heart. "He found you," he said to them, patient of cruel illusion, of anything that gave him their likenesses, even if it mocked him in the gift.

"What *are* you?" Jillan said, driving the dagger deeper. There was panic in her voice.

"Don't be afraid," Rafe said. But Paul went out—*out,* like the extinguishing of a light, and Jillan backed away, shaking her head at his offered hand.

"No," she said. "No." And fled, raced ghostlike through the wall.

His own doppelganger still stood there, naked, hands empty at his sides, with anguish in his eyes.

"I tried," the doppelganger said with a motion of his hand. "I tried. Rafe—they'll come back. Sooner or later they'll have to come back. There's nowhere else to go."

Rafe sank down where he stood, where a node made a sitting-place against the wall. He ached in every bone and muscle, and looked up at the doppelganger in unadulterated misery.

"Rafe," the doppelganger said. "I think they're dead. You understand me? They haven't found anything of themselves. I'm not sure there's anything left to find."

Rafe shut his eyes, willing it all away; but the doppelganger had come closer when he opened them. It knelt in front of him, waiting, his own face projecting grief and sympathy back at him.

"You understand?" the doppelganger said. "They're copies. That's all I found. They're like me."

He wanted to scream at it to go away, to be silent, but a strange self-courtesy held him still to listen, to sit calmly with his hands on his knees and stare into his own face, knowing the doppelganger's pain, knowing it to the height and depth, what it cost and how it hurt. *Jillan dead. And Paul.* He had known it in his heart for hours, that this place, this graveyard caricature of *Lindy* had all the important pieces in it. The console. The EVApod. Himself. All the working salvage that was left. "Do they know?" he asked, half insane himself.

"I can't tell." The image remained kneeling there. "On the one hand they could be right; they thought—they thought this was illusion. Maybe it is. But it was too strong a one for them."

"It's not illusion."

"I don't think so either."

"God, this is mad!"

"I know. I know it is. But I think you're right. We split—I remember all this pain. I remember—these arms waving about. It hurt, I never remember any pain like that—"

"Cut it out."

"I think—that was where they died."

"Shut up!"

That Rafe tucked up his knees, rested his forehead on his arms—grief incarnate, mirror of his own, mirror until it hurt to look at himself, knowing what he felt, seeing it mimed in front of him. Rafe Two lifted his head at last, stared at him with ineffable bleakness, and he began to shiver himself in long slow tremors.

"Cry," the soft voice came to him. "I did, awhile, for what it's worth. I cried a lot. But it can't change what is. Don't you think I want to believe you're not real? That we're all of us all right? I wish I could believe that. You wish you could get rid of me. But you can't. And we aren't."

"Damn you!" He leaped up, ran to the console, seized on the first thing he could find and flung it at the doppelganger. It was one of his music tapes, which passed through the image and hit the wall, falling harmless as the curse; and the doppleganger just sat there, breathing, doing everything it should not. Its breath came hard, one long heave of its naked shoulders, its head bowed as if it fought for self-control. It mastered itself, better than he; or having fewer options. It was resignation that looked back at him with his own face, out of bruised and weary eyes, and he could not bear that defeat. He sank down at the console and gasped for air that seemed too thin, with thoughts that seemed too rarified to hold without suffocating. Things swirled about him: *Dead, dead, dead—*

Die too, why can't you?

He did not cry. Sitting there, he shivered until his muscles ached and cramped, until lack of air brought him to bow his head on the console.

"He's real," he heard his own voice say; and Jillan's then: "No," so that he opened his eyes and found them standing there, all of them, his dead, his living self—

"O God," he said, "God, Jillan, Paul—don't go, don't go this time." He levered himself up, unsteady on his feet, offered them his hand, even knowing they could not touch it. "Stay here. Don't run."

His doppelganger walked to him, stood close by him, ghostly thin, standing where he stood in parodied embrace. There was no sensation from it, only a confusion of image, as if it had superimposed itself deliberately.

"Don't go," it echoed him. "Don't you see—we're the illusion. Projected here. We're androids. That's all we are. Made out of him, his mind, Jillan's, Paul's. We're the shadows. He's the real one."

They stood there, the two of them, staring at him. "It doesn't make sense," Jillan said in a small voice. "Rafe—we can't be dead. Can we?"

Rafe himself sank down to his knees on the gossamer-covered carpet, squeezed his eyes shut and shook his head to clear it of all the accumulated lunacy.

"I think," said the other Rafe, standing over him, about him, a moving pale shimmer—"I think it's very likely, if we can't find the bodies. I think you are."

"Then what are we?" Paul yelled.

"Androids," said Rafe Two. "Something like that, at least. They made us. And the originals are gone." He walked over near the console, touched the edges of the seats with insubstantial fingers. "We never rigged *Lindy* for much stress."

"Something that they made," Jillan said. "Is that what you're saying?"

"Yes," Rafe said, himself, looking up at her from where he knelt.

She was still in every particular his sister, that look, that quiet steady sense. It shattered him. "Yes. Something that they made."

She stared in his direction a moment, then shrugged and laughed, taking a step away. "I don't *feel* dead." A second step, so that she began to fade out at the wall. "I'm going out of focus, aren't I?" Soberly, with horror beneath the surface. "It's a pretty good copy. Aren't I?"

"Stop it!" Paul said.

"Jillan's right," Rafe Two said, by the EVApod. "It was the seats, understand? We never rigged for more than two or three G at most. We got a lot more than that. It flung us off. Remember? Autopilot went crazy. My fault, maybe. But I couldn't stop us. Nothing could, our tanks depleted—Couldn't if we'd had *Lindy* at max. *Lindy* couldn't cope with it."

"We're not dead," Paul said.

"Whatever we are," Rafe Two said, folding his insubstantial arms, "I guess we don't have that problem. Not anymore we don't."

"We aren't dead!"

"Let be," Rafe said, hating his own tendencies to push a thing. Paul hated to be pushed.

"We're us-prime," Jillan said. "That's what we are." She came and squatted near him, looking at him closely for the first time, her hands clasped together on her knees, her knees drawn up. "I wish you could lend me a blanket, brother."

"I wish I could," he said. "Are you cold?" That she should be cold seemed to him the last, unbearable cruelty.

She shook her head. "Just the indignity of the thing. I tell you, when we meet what did this to us, when we meet them, I'll sure insist on my clothes back."

"I'll insist on more than that," he said.

"You've already met it!" Paul shouted, over by the wall. *"That's* Rafe—the one like us! Ask it where we are. Ask it what kind of jokes it likes to play, what it's up to, where it came from, what it wants from us!"

"I'm alive," Rafe said.

"He's the one that bleeds," said his doppelganger, from close by. "Look at his face. He's the one that survived the wreck. Not a mark on any of the rest of us—is there?" Rafe Two squatted down nearby, elbows on his knees. "At least," he said to Jillan's wraith, "you've got title to a name. Rafe and I—we aren't the same anymore, not quite. We split. He's been alone and I've been chasing you, and on that reckoning we get less and less in step, while you—you *are* his sister, much as mine; you took up where the other left off—permanently. And so did you, Paul. That's why it seems to you you're still alive. But I can tell myself apart from him. I'm Rafe who found that one lying unconscious on the floor; and he's the one who met himself face to face awake. Different perspectives. Dead's meaningless to you. You're not that Jillan Murray; you're her hypothesis, you're what she would have done—being met with that place where we woke up. You're not that Paul Gaines. You're just living your present on his memories— the way I split off from his, and did things different than he did."

Paul came slowly away from the wall, stood there and shook his head. "I won't give in to this. You're wrong."

"At least," Rafe said, "sit down. Sit down. Please."

"It's dark out there," said Paul, as if it were a matter of petulant complaint.

"Rafe said," Rafe answered him. "Stay here. Please."

Paul came and joined them, farthest away, crouched on the floor and plucked disinterestedly at a shred of gossamer he failed even to touch.

"We're interested in the same things, aren't we?" Rafe said. "We're still partners. We need to find out where we are. And I love you," he added, because it was so, and he had not said it often enough. He remembered what he was talking to, but it was as close as he could come. "I do love you two. . . ."—To convince himself, he thought.

"I know," Jillan said. Her eyes were dreadful, as if they saw too much. "I know that, Rafe."

"Nothing for me," said Rafe Two, who sat by him mirrorlike, arms about naked knees. "You see what it is to be surplus? Better to be dead. At least there's appreciation."

"Shut it up," Rafe said. "I always had a bad sense of timing. I won't put up with it from you."

"*Stop it!*" Paul said.

"It's like being schizophrenic," Rafe said, looking at the floor, pulling with his fingers at another loose bit of gossamer that refused to tear. "It's really strong, this stuff."

"What are we going to do?" Jillan asked.

"I don't see any profit in sitting still," Paul said. "Do you?"

"What do you suggest? It—they—whatever—whatever runs this place knows where we are. When it gets bored, it'll find us."

Paul glared at him.

"I don't want to sit here," Jillan said.

"There's the corridors," said Rafe Two. "We could try to go as far as we can. As far as we can stay with each other."

"We could try that," Rafe said.

The outsiders moved slowly down the corridor which had been allotted to them and there was, immediately, throughout the ship, a focusing of attention.

"They're a hazard," [] said. [] had tried them once, but $<>$ had interfered in no uncertain terms and [] kept respectful distance.

"Let them go," said $<\wedge>$. $<\wedge>$ was constantly disposed to gentleness. It was part of $<\wedge>$'s madness, forgetting $<\wedge>$'s heredity.

But $</>$ ranged all about the perimeters, gathering others of $</>$'s disposition: there were many such aboard. There were two or three fiercer, but none more devious, except maybe the segments of $=<->==<+>=$ that grew longer with every cannibalistic acquisition. $=<->==<+>1g=$ had fifteen other segments, currently at liberty, and it was a question where these were or what the whole matrix thought, breaking apart and sending segments of itself everywhere in search of information.

$</>$ laughed to $</>$self, loving chaos, seeing opportunity.

Trishanamarandu-kepta devoted only a part of $<>$'s mind to this maneuvering. There were other things to occupy $<>$'s mind, a wealth of things the little ship had given up, records, names.

Of the simulacra themselves, three templates existed, which were deliberately dissociated in fragments.

From those templates $<>$ integrated three temporary copies.

Rafe waked, aware of nakedness, of dark, of Paul and Jillan close beside him.

He wept, recalling pain, got to his knees and shook at Jillan's bare shoulder. "Jillan," he said.

The eyes opened, fixed. Jillan began to tremble, to convulse in spasms, to scream long tearing screams.

"Jillan!" Rafe yelled, trying to hold her. Paul was awake too, trying to restrain her and evade her blows.

These were temporary copies, easily erased, and served as comparison against which < >'s own symbol systems could be examined.

< > tried one on. It proved difficult, and retreated into gibberish; < > shut it down.

There remained Rafe and Jillan. The one called Rafe seemed the easiest of entry. The most stable seemed Jillan, and < > shut Rafe-mind down for the moment, to consider Jillan's, which bent and flexed and made defensive mazes of its workings—giving way quickly and then proving vastly resilient.

"Rafe," Jillan cried as they waked together in this dark place, and Rafe stared at her, leaning backward on his arms, seeming unable to do more than shiver. "There was—" he said, started to say, and cried out and fell back.

"Rafe!" she cried, and shook at him, but he was loose as if someone had broken him, and then he went away, just vanished, as if he had never been.

"Rafe!" she screamed at the vacant air, at the ceiling, and the dark. *"Paul!"* She scrambled up and threatened the invisible with empty hands and great violence.

It would fight, this Jillan-mind. < > learned that. The passengers who hovered near to witness this were profoundly disturbed.

"< > is taking risks again," </ > whispered in far recesses of the ship. "One day < > will miscalculate. Remember = = = = before = = = = turned cannibal? < > did not foresee that either."

< > ignored these whispers, being occupied with < >'s insertion into the Jillan-mind.

Who are you? Jillan-mind asked < >. She wept; she fought the intrusions and when she no longer could do that she took in the flood with the peculiar strength she had and started trying to bend it to her shape.

She looked at $</>$, which had come to hover near, and bent $<>$'s thoughts to notice the observer in the dark.

"I don't trust that one," she declared, and $<>$ laughed for startlement, in the rest of $<>$'s mind, which went on seeing things from outside, and managing $<>$'s body, and doing the other things $<>$ did in the normal course of $<>$'s existence.

Then $<>$ moved in Jillan-mind abruptly and without gentleness. $<>$ brushed aside defenses and began to take what $<>$ wanted. Jillan screamed at $<>$ in anger and in pain and finally, because $<>$ filled all the pathways of her mind at once and ran out of storage, the scream changed character and reason.

$<>$ meddled with this state for a moment, adjusting this, tampering with that. $<>$ had known already that the storage was not adequate and now $<>$ formed strategies, knowing the dimensions of what $<>$ had. The pain went on, while $<>$ probed connections and relationships.

Jillan stabilized again, regarded the dark and welcomed it with fierce enthusiasm and hunger.

$<>$ erased her then abruptly, for she had gotten far from the template, and ceased to be instructive. Or safe. In any sense.

$<>$ made a second, fresher copy. $<>$ could do that endlessly, in possession of the templates $<>$ had made.

$<>$ began again, with a surer, more knowing touch.

"Is it worth it?" $<*>$ asked, straying close. "Let this creature go."

$<>$ turned the Jillan-face toward $<*>$'s undisguised self and felt a jolt of horror and of sound.

"That was unkind," $<>$ said, and destroyed her yet again.

"You'll have to wait," Rafe said, in their trek through endless corridors of endless green-gossamer and lumpish contours. Nothing had changed. They discovered nothing but endless sameness. He sank down, resting his back against the wall, and shut his eyes—opened them again for fear of finding himself alone, but the images stayed with him. They had sat down as if they needed to, Rafe Two foremost, always closest to him. He heaved a breath, felt his bruised ribs creak, felt thirst and hunger. Tears leaked unwanted from his eyes, simple exhaustion, and horror at the sameness and the sight that kept staring back at him.

Ghosts. Solemn Rafe; Jillan being nonchalant; Paul glowering—
they frightened him. He could not touch them. He could not hug them
to him, ever again. He knew those looks—Paul's when he had an idea
and would not let it go, Jillan's when she was on the edge and totter-
ing.

"Come on," he said, "Jillan. Swear. Do something. Don't be cheer-
ful at me."

Her face settled into something true and dour. She looked up at
him, thinking—

—thinking what? he wondered. Seeing aliens behind his eyes? Or
feeling her own death again?

"You all right?" he asked.

"Sure, sure I'm all right," Jillan said, and looked about, redirecting
what got uncomfortable. "Whatever designed this place was crazy,
you know that?"

"Whatever keeps us here sure is," Rafe Two said.

"It keeps me alive," Rafe answered the doppelganger. He wiped at
his mouth, looked up and down the windings of the corridor—they
had gone down this time, if the large chamber had been up. "That it
leaves me alone, you know, is something encouraging."

"There's another place," said Rafe Two. "It's dark, and nothing,
and if that's its normal condition, that thing's nothing like us at all."

"It's playing games," Paul said; and Rafe looked at him with some
little hope—*it*, then; Paul had stopped throwing that *it* at him, had
perhaps reconceived his situation. "There's no guarantee it has a logic,
you figure that?"

"It's got math; math's logic," Jillan said.

"A lunatic can add," Paul said, gnawing at his lip. "I don't get
tired. You're sweating and I don't get tired."

"Dead has advantages, it seems," Rafe Two said.

"Shut up!"

"Try thinking," Rafe said, shifting to thrust a leg between his doppelganger and Paul's image. "Try thinking—how we go about talking
to this thing. It tried to talk to us. Back there—at Endeavor, it made
an approach. Maybe taking us was a mistake in the first place."

"Come on," said Jillan harshly. "It knew we were there, knew how
small we were. We couldn't support jump engines. It damn well
knew."

He blinked at his sister, felt the sweat running in his eyes, mortality that she was beyond feeling. "I'll find a way to ask it," he said. Of a sudden he wanted to cry, right there in front of them, as if the jolt had just gotten through to him, but all he managed was a little trickle from his eyes and a painful jerk of breath. "I'll tell you this. If it turns out the way you think and you can't get your hands on it, I'll get it. I'll go for it. You can believe I will."

"I've thought of something else," said Rafe Two.

"What's that?"

"That offending it might turn us off. That it can do that anyway when it wants."

"What he's saying," Jillan said, "is that it has us for hostages. And maybe it's not being whimsical with us. Maybe it's looking to learn— oh, basic things. Like how we build; what our logic's like—"

"—from *Lindy*'s wire and bolts," Rafe scoffed. "Lord, it'll wonder how we got to space at all."

"—our language; our little computer, simple as it is—"

"—how our minds work," said Paul. "They'll start prodding at us. They've kept us too—you figure that, Rafe? They've gone to a lot of trouble."

"It still could be," Rafe said, "what you might say . . . humanitarian concern. Maybe they panicked and bolted and we were an unwanted attachment."

"How long were you awake?" Paul asked. "I *died.*" His voice went faint; the muscles of his insubstantial face shook and jerked with such semblance of life it jarred. *"I am dead.* Isn't that what you've been insisting? I remember what it did. I remember the pain, Rafe. And it wasn't any damn humanitarian concern."

Rafe sat and stared at him, looked away finally, for Paul had begun to cry and to wipe his eyes, and finally faded out on them.

Jillan went after that, just winked out.

"How do you do that?" Rafe asked his double, hollow to the heart. "Where do you go when you go out? That dark place?"

"Don't get superstitious about it. It's just a place, that's all. You think hard about it—I think we've got a simple off-on with a transmitter somewhere."

"It wouldn't be simple."

"Bad choice of words."

"Dammit, I don't like arguing with you. It gives me the shakes."

"You ever wonder how I found you," Rafe Two asked, waving a hand toward the vastness of the hall, "in all this? Coincidence?"

"Something's pushing the buttons."

"Don't put it that way," Rafe Two said and hunched his bare shoulders, hands tucked between his knees. "You make me nervous, twin."

"You scared of dying?"

Rafe Two nodded, slowly, simply. "So are they, I think. Jillan and Paul. They've got experience."

"I'm hungry. My knees ache. Do yours?"

"No body left—brother. Got nothing like that left to bother me." The eyes were his own, and worried. "I'm going to go after them."

"Don't leave me here!"

Rafe Two looked at him. "It'll see we get back together. Won't it?"

"I have to go back to the ship. I have to. We're gaining nothing out here wandering these passages. Get them back. Come back yourself. To the ship. When you can."

"The ship." The doppelganger gave a dry and bitter laugh. "It won't let you lose that either, will it?"

"I'm afraid for them."

"So am I."

The doppelganger left, a winking-out more abrupt than Paul's.

So there had been violent parting of the ways; one fled: two gave chase; the living one pursued a painful trek back, < > surmised, to origins.

"</ > is gathering malcontents," said =(+)=, on leave from its cannibalistic whole.

< > was amused, with that part of < >'s attention it had to spare. *Trishanamarandu-kepta* rode inertia at the moment. < > had figured (accurately thus far) that this carbon-life, having ships capable of FTL, having the tendency to cluster together as they seemed to do, would not disperse themselves in long solitary voyages in between the stars and points of mass, so this vacancy seemed a likely place to coast undisturbed. < > preferred a few problems at a time: there were the passengers, after all, who were disturbed enough at three outsiders in their midst. So < > did not court attack from this carbon-life at large.

The species might, < > judged, with the example of Jillan-mind, be very quick to attack if it had the chance.

< > was learning things. Jillan-mind and Rafe-mind in particular were responsive to the logic < > discovered in the primitive machinery, while Paul-mind refused focus, being a flood of strong responses on every level. They were not structurally the same, but there were strong similarities. Conclusions suggested themselves, but < > did not rush headlong into judgment, having wide experience which made surmise both slow and elaborate.

Throughout the ship other passengers were waking, more and more of them during this interlude, some of which had not waked in a very long time. Often they blundered into the barriers < > had made. But nothing got into the area where the visitors were at liberty.

This defense < > managed with one part of < >'s mind, and used another small probe on the Jillan-consciousness.

< > erased one temporary image, which began to disintegrate in subtle ways; but it was no effort now to enter the Jillan-mind on the level < > had already achieved, and < > integrated another.

Trishanamarandu-kepta had found a large bit of debris, meanwhile, and stored it for conversion, as it dealt with dust and interstellar hydrogen. < > constantly attended such things.

< > called up the Rafe-mind, and probed him with some sophistication, seeking out the differences, both physical and otherwise.

Rafe was, < > decided, less resilient but more stubborn. His barriers lasted longer, and snapped with a suddenness and disintegration that made < > suspect for a moment < > had met some clever trap, so disorienting and painful the reaction.

It was shock, < > decided. Rafe-mind had simply no experience with losing on that level, and he had met defeat without expectation, absolute and devastating, when he had planned to endure pain and outwait it.

From this collapse, Rafe-mind did not reintegrate, though < > observed him patiently and gave him every chance. So he would perish, ultimately. < > destroyed him and recreated him afresh.

It was paradoxical defense at best. It hinted irrationalities, capacities that would be augmented by physical systems in the living one, and Rafe himself had been, < > thought, stunned by his own failure.

< > suspected then why this one had survived in physical form, and why < > had so quickly broken him.

< > had robbed him of motives, that was what. That was why Rafe-mind had come apart, in solitude, without the other two.

< > did not intend Rafe-mind to learn this about himself, not yet.

Distress continued among the three newcomers. The simulacra which had gotten loose ran at hazard through their confinement, emitting terror as they went.

Paul, < > thought; it would of course be Paul in the lead, and < > was right in < >'s assessment, < > discovered, reaching out to prevent him from a meeting with = = = =, which lurked in anticipation.

= = = = was outraged. But < > pent Paul Gaines safely out of harm's way, diverted Jillan elsewhere, and established barriers in haste, having < >'s mind on a dozen other matters.

"Robber!" = = = = hissed.

"Out," said < >. And = = = = went, calling in = = = ='s segments that were still at large. Most howled in protest. But they came. And the idle curious scattered.

Trishanamarandu-kepta found a second bit of rock, and sucked that down as well, while automata attended small repairs.

< > considered *Lindy* with another part of < >'s large mind, its structures, its simplicity, for < > had not yet sent the mote to feed *Trishanamarandu-kepta's* needs. It might. But < > thus far refrained, finding interest in it.

Then because Paul continued to batter himself unreasoningly at the barriers, < > gave Paul a Rafe-simulacrum to keep him calm and let him wonder why that Rafe should be difficult to wake. Paul shook at him and wept and cursed. That, < > judged, would keep him out of mischief.

For more immediate purposes < > chose the Jillan-face.

Chapter Five

Rafe went striding through the dark, calling Jillan and Paul by name, tireless in his pace and wishing desperately that endurance made some difference—for they would not grow tired here any more than he would, and he could not overtake them by all the laws he knew of this place. He could never overtake them until one of them came to his senses and stopped.

Paul was running; that was what Rafe guessed, running in hurt and fear. Paul had always been the gentle one, the little boy who had played at explorer and shuddered at the dark—

—*Space frightens me,* Paul had confessed to him once. *I'm all right in ships; just keep walls around me. When I have to go EVA, I just keep looking at the ship, the rock, whatever. Give me boundaries.*

Paul was station-born. He had a stationer's way of looking at things, and large concepts got to him, like the idea of staring time in the face when he looked out at the stars. The inside-out of jump frightened him. There were dimensions of time and space Paul staunchly refused to believe in, or at least to think of, even while he used and traveled through them.

I'm not dead, Paul had insisted; Paul Gaines could not die; no stationer could be so much alone as that. The universe would not permit so gross a violence to the devoutly nonviolent.

"Paul," Rafe called, aching for him. His own ill-timed joking, his bloody sense of humor, the other Rafe's—Paul did not support the contradictions. "Paul! Jillan, come back!"

Eventually a light came toward him, looking like a star at first, then a figure walking with that gliding, too-rapid stride that was the law within this place.

It was Jillan, by herself.

"Where's Paul?" he shouted at her, but Jillan kept coming without answering, and that silence chilled him, intimating that something dire had happened—Jillan, without Paul.

Her face was dreadful when they met, her eyes vast and shadowed, and again the illogicity of themselves overwhelmed him, that whatever they were could suffer—*Have we flesh of a kind,* he wondered, *bodies somewhere, beyond this dark? Metal bodies standing in a row or going through pointless motions? O Paul, Jillan—*

"Where's Paul?" he asked his sister.

"R-r-r-aaa-ffe," the lips shaped, a hoarse, rasping effort with Jillan's voice. It reached for him.

"O God. God, no!" He flung himself back and ran with all his might.

He hit a barrier, not a hard one, but a slowing of his force until he could not move more than a few feet in any direction. He felt a touch on his shoulders. He turned and met Jillan's eyes, encountered its embrace.

It was strong, stronger than he was by far. "Let me go," he cried, and struck at this thing, beyond any fear of harming Jillan. *"Let her go, damn you!"*

It hugged him to its heart. *"R-r-raaa-ffffe,"* it said, handling him with irresistible force, as if he had been a child in Jillan's arms.

He screamed, yelled out names—his own was one—*"Rafe!"* as if his other self could hear him, help him, at least know that he was lost.

Jillan carried him some distance and stopped at last, just stopped, and let him go. *Free,* he thought, having wild hope of escape. He flung himself away as she winked out, but he came up against a barrier, solid as a wall.

Pain hit, and he screamed and went on screaming, from shock at first, and then because he could not stop.

"Rafe," he heard Jillan say out of a vast void darkness; and he waked again, blind and numb at first, lying on nothing, face up? face down?

Then Jillan was by him, kneeling there bright with gold-green glow, with seeming tears glistening in her eyes and spilling down her face. He felt her hands as she shook at him. "Come on, Rafe, wake up, you've got to wake up, hear me?"

He moved: he could, and writhed out of her reach, sat there shivering and staring back at her.

"Paul's lost," she said in a hoarse and hollow voice.

He shivered then, not for Paul, whose fate seemed a thousand years ago to him; but for himself, for the inexplicable that happened to him and went on happening in this blind dark.

"We've got to get back," he said at last, for it was truly Jillan. He convinced himself it was. He forced sense past numb lips, going on living, desperately ignoring memory as something unmanageable. "We've got to get back to the ship, tell *him*—" as if his living half would know what to do, would have some holistic view he lacked. He no longer trusted himself or anything he saw. He had dreamed his kidnapping. He had dreamed the pain. He wanted to believe in none of it. "Jillan—how did you find me?"

"I just kept walking back," she said. "Paul's *lost*. He's out there somewhere and he's not answering or something's happened to him—"

Something happened to me, he started to tell her, facing her hysteria; and some reticence held the truth dammed up. It was Jillan. He kept looking for flaws and cracks, but it was indeed his sister. He had to believe it was. "Let's get out of here," he said, not wanting to be touched by her, not wanting to look in her eyes. *Have you met something too?* he wanted to ask. *Have you already met it?*

Is it somewhere still inside you?

Is it alive in me?

"I've tried to get out," she said.

"What do you mean, tried to get out?"

She nodded toward the dark in general, or in a particular direction. "A few paces off—there's just a wall." She hugged her knees against her, tight, muscles rigid in her arms. "It's got us penned here. That's what."

He stood up and tried, all round, but it was like hitting some painless wall of force, insubstantial and absolute at once. He battered it with his fist, and his arm simply stopped short, impotent and forceless.

"*Aaaaaaiiiiiieeeeeee!*" something wailed, just the other side.

"God!" he said, and staggered back, crouched down in primate tuck, shoulders hunched, facing the barrier with Jillan at his back. He felt vulnerable so, deliberately kept staring into the dark, determined to believe in her, that it *was* Jillan behind him.

Sister, he thought, *sister.* They had called him the Old Man, she had. Paul had. The thinker, captain, planner, head-of-family, for all he was only twenty-two. He had outright failed them, all down the line; and he saw it now, how they had looked to him, Paul in his way, Jillan in hers, because he told her he could do it all for her and Paul, and she trusted that he could. She handed her life and future to him—*Here, brother, I've got what I need; I've got Paul: you take us, and do something, making something of yourself and us—*

—merchanter-man, who was nothing without his ship, his sister to give it children—

He was not sure of Jillan now. He was not sure of Paul. If Jillan was truly gone nothing mattered, not even Paul.

But he would, he discovered, go on fighting, as long as it was not Jillan herself who struck the blow. Being a merchanter brat, he had a certain stubbornness: that was all he could call it at this point, a certain rock-hardness at the center that did not know where to quit.

Not revenge. That was nothing. It was Murray-stubbornness, that lasted through the War, the mines, *Lindy*'s making, the Belt. He had always wondered if there was anything in him but Jillan.

Now he knew.

And he was, he thought with a jolt that ached, only the merest shadow of the man. The real substance of him was back in the lighted corridor, waiting for him, depending on him.

Two of us, he thought, and it occurred to him that, being Old Man, he still had one living crewman to protect. He was father to one at least. Himself.

"Rafe's our business," he said to Jillan at his back. "You understand me. Not me-Rafe. The other one. They can still hurt him. We've got to do something."

"You got an idea?" she asked. No protest. That other Rafe was her brother too, the living one. "You got an idea?"

"No," he said, "just a priority. Paul's no worse off than we are. No better either. But our brother—" It was easier to think of Rafe that way. "They're going to some trouble in his case. They saw to it that we found him. Didn't they? That wasn't accident."

"There's still the outside chance, like Rafe says—they're not altogether hostile. Maybe we can't figure the way they think. Maybe they're too different."

He twisted on his knees and looked back at her, snatching up a hope from that innocence of events. "I met one," he said. "It wore your shape."

Jillan blinked rapidly in shock, stared at him, seeming then to put things together.

"I figure you'd better know that," he said, "so you don't trust everything you see. It hurt. Quite a bit. Like at the beginning. It's still got us here, wherever here is."

The shock was real in her eyes. He saw that.

"Paul and Rafe," she said, putting that together too. "It can get at them that way."

$< >$ was pleased in $< >$'s acquisition. It had been a question whether to shock Rafe Two with any kind of contact, any apprehension at all of his circumstances before securing his template, but $< >$ had decided in the affirmative. The second Rafe-mind's difference was precisely, after all, its knowledge, its adjustment to the environment more extensive than Rafe One's. And the Jillan-face provided a certain insulation in the contact.

$< >$ tried out what $< >$ had gained, this Rafe with a little bit of knowledge where he was and what he was. The flexibility was greater. $< >$ had hoped for that.

The solitude was worst, the long, gnawing away of expectations until the loss of the most dreadful fear seemed like the parting of a cherished possession, leaving increasingly remote and strange possibilities.

One could only pace so much, eat so often, meddle with the few active circuits *Lindy* had left just so many hours, and bathe and sleep and bathe and sleep and make-work at the console, like the visual analysis of stars, the infinite working of infinite problems, calculation of space and acceleration and distances given things that would never, from his vantage, ever be true. But those hypotheses filled the mind and kept it focused, for a little while, on sane outcomes.

Rafe worked at guesses, had pegged several high-magnitude stars, two of which were conspicuous, almost touching. He tried one and another theoretical perspective on them, tormented himself with hopeful and despairing suppositions.

"Hey!" he shouted at the winding corridor more than once, frustrated and desperate. But no sound came back, from either direction.

He called the others' names; he called his own, and had nothing but silence.

"You can't take them away," he muttered to himself, to God, to whatever ran this place, and bowed his head on the console. Finally, which he had never yet done, he truly mourned his dead and sobbed hysterically.

Even that wore thin. There was only so much grief, so much anger, not even so much as when he and Jillan were orphaned. Then there had been guilt—a child's kind of guilt—*Maybe if I'd been good they'd be alive—*

It's my fault. I should have loved them more—

There was no guilt here. Not with Jillan and Paul. He sat there with the last of the tears still cold on his face and judged that whatever mistakes they had made, they were paying for all of it together; Jillan and Paul's being dead was not final but drawn-out, shared, a life-in-death which still could make jokes about its state, shed tears for itself, know fears for the future. The same thing waited for him, he reckoned, when whatever-it-was got around to his case.

It's going to do that soon; they don't want to watch what happens to me.

Or maybe they're just gone. Turned off, of no more use.

No pain that way, at least.

And at last, all but sobbing in self-pity, he thought: *But Rafe's afraid to die.*

He shuddered away from that entanglement and wiped his face with both his hands until the tears went down.

He thought of taking another long, long walk. His bruises had gone to livid green by now. He was stronger. He might take food, fill his pockets with it, use a plastic bag for a canteen—just walk, walk until he ran out of everything and those in charge had to do something about him, either meet him face to face or let him die.

But: *Come to the ship,* he had told his doppelganger. Perhaps their time sense was different. Maybe for them it was only a little while. If he left they might come and he would never know.

He flung himself down against the wall where he often sat and just stared at *Lindy*'s remains, not looking down the corridors which led into the dark.

"Rafe," his own voice said.

He started half to his feet, braced against the wall, levered himself the rest of the way up. "Where have *you* been?" It came out harsh. He had not meant that. He was all but shaking, facing his naked self, which stood over against the dark of the corridor. "Did you find them?"

"Were you worried?"

"Was I worried? Don't joke with me, man. I'm not laughing. Where are they?"

The doppelganger pointed, vaguely up and off beyond the walls. "There."

"They won't come?"

"Paul's not coping well with this."

He let go his breath, found his hands shaking, walked over to the console and sat down, firmly, in a place he knew. "Not coping well."

"Not at all."

"Jillan?"

"Better. She's all right."

"She's with him."

The doppelganger shook his head. "No. She's not."

"Cut the riddles. Where's Jillan?"

"You're upset."

"God, what's wrong—*wrong with you?*"

"Nothing's wrong."

"I know what it's like—talking to myself; I do know; and you don't follow my lead, not half right—" He put himself on his feet, leaning on *Lindy*'s board. *"What are you?"*

The doppelganger winked out.

"What are you?" Rafe screamed after it. He hit the useless board. *"Jil-lan!"*

And he sat down again, fell into his seat, trembling from head to foot.

"Clever," said the doppelganger voice, off to his side.

He spun the chair, faced it where he sat. It stood over by the EVApod, dimmer, for the light was brighter there.

"You," he said to it, gathering up his mind, "you're the one I've been wanting to get in reach. Why don't you come in here in person?"

"You want to kill me."

"Maybe." He sucked in a copper-edged breath and stood up. "Where's my sister? Where's Paul?"

"The physical entities? Dead. I tried to hold them. They died."

"Dead. And their copies—" He did not want to admit how much it meant, but his knees were weak. He held onto the counter. "Do they still exist?"

"Oh, yes."

"Bring them here."

"I'll let them loose again. Soon. I came to talk with you."

"Why?" he asked, staring at the mirrored face before the blank visage of the EVApod. "To say what? What shape is Rafe going to be in? Do I get my own doppelganger back?"

"Yes. He's safe. Is that a concern to you?"

He did not answer. It already knew weaknesses enough in him; it wore his doppelganger like a skin. He straightened his back and moved back to the console, turned around again. "Why not your own shape?"

"It would distress you."

"You think this doesn't?"

"A question of degree."

"You're not very like us."

"No. I'm not."

"You're fluent."

The image blinked. "It did take time."

"How did you do it? How did you learn?"

"It would distress you. Say that I know you pretty well. From inside. I have a lot of your character right now."

"And my memories?"

"That too."

Rafe sank again into the chair, wiped a hand across his mouth to still the tic that plagued him. "And the way I think about things. I don't suppose you've got that too."

"There is a great deal of congruency at present. I've walled off some of myself; that's the nearest analogue. I'm larger. Smarter. Far more educated."

"Modest too."

The doppelganger grinned.

"God," Rafe said, "a sense of humor." It sent a chill up his back, lent him other thoughts. "You can feel anything I'd feel. Do you?"

"Everything."

"Like—loving them. Like that."

"I do."

He sat silent a moment, trying not to shiver.

"While I'm you," it said. "In my full mind there are other considerations, I assure you. But within this configuration, I do love them. I understand perfectly what you mean."

"You hurt us. Do you know that?"

"You can assume I remember. You don't have to ask. You're concerned about your safety, about the others. Let me destroy your illusions—"

"Don't. Please. Don't."

"Not those." The mouth twisted in a smile that left no residue of humor. "Not physically. . . ."

</> had made a move. In the rest of < >'s mind, extended elsewhere in the ship, < > was well aware of this. </> gained access to apparatus </> could not otherwise have touched, and </> grew suddenly knowledgeable. It was the file on the intruders </> had gotten. </> gained sudden capability.

"Help," (#) cried, rushing through the ship. "Help, help!"

"I told you so," said <ˆ>.

". . . but I won't tell you any more than you really have to know, if you'd rather not. I do mean to take you back."

"Where?"

"To the star where I found you."

"Is this a game?" Rafe's heart was beating hard. "Why? Why do that?"

"A capsule with a beacon. They'll pick you up, so this mind believes."

"Why go to the trouble?"

"Why not? Harm to me? I don't think they could."

"You're lying."

There was long silence. "I understand your caution. Believe me. I do understand."

"More humor."

The mouth—his own—quirked up in a touch of mirth. "It doesn't depend on your belief anyway."

"You mean you'll do what you like."

"Aaaaiiiiiiiiii!" The sound began from far away; it roared closer and closer, speakers coming alive right overhead and fading away again, lightning-fast, blinding pain that hit and left: Rafe leaped up, trembling in its wake.

"Is that for effect?"

"That one's mad," the doppelganger said. "And a little upset right now. Don't let it trouble you."

"Sure. Sure I won't. Cheap trick, hear? Like all the rest. Real cheap."

"I'll leave now. Something wants my attention. A minor thing. But I'll put in somewhere soon at a human port and drop you off. Don't worry for the jump drugs. I don't know the composition of what you take. You don't. But I can make you sleep; that should be enough."

"Why does it matter? You've killed two people, damn you! Why does it matter now?"

"Because it's easy," the doppelganger said, and faded out altogether.

"Why?" he yelled after it until his voice cracked. He fell down into

the chair, being alone again, in the silence. "Rafe?" he said aloud, querulously, hoping for the old one, the friendly one. "Jillan?" And last and with least hope: "Paul?"

No one answered. No one came. He was scared finally, finally terrified for himself, sitting and staring at nothing at all.

Going home, he thought. With human beings. Living ones. He did not believe it. He did not believe it loved. He did not believe it told the truth at all, or that it cared.

But there remained the possibility.

There remained the greater likelihood it had other motives. And it wore a human shape and used a human mind.

"Paul," </> said, having penetrated the barriers <> had imposed about the stranger, having, momentarily, seized control of that territory. "Paul."

And </> took the Rafe-image on </>self.

"You're awake," Paul said. "You're awake."

"Paul," </> said, getting to </>'s human feet. "Paul." </> had that word down pat. </> snatched Paul in </>'s borrowed arms and carried him rapidly out through barriers, along passages.

Paul screamed, and stopped screaming, simply clinging to what he feared, a logic that </>, in Rafe's mind, understood with curious poignancy.

<> was too late to prevent the theft.

<> simply recreated the Paul-simulacrum of which <> had been robbed and left him asleep in a safer place, far inside <>'s boundaries.

Paul was not a serious loss. Paul had never adjusted and likely never would, but <> was still nettled.

"<> wish you success," <> taunted </>, for <> had shed the Rafe-mind and felt differently about many things.

There was a division in *Trishanamarandu-kepta*. It had happened long ago. There was a place where </> did very much as </> pleased; and another where <> was the law. This was an agreement they had, one which made diversions, and <> cherished those.

Slowly, as <>'s humor improved, <> found a sense of ironical amusement in the theft, for the Paul-entity was unstable; and the

Rafe-one had been unwaked and was now vastly disturbed. One did not intrude into a simulacrum and leave it intact.

"Do something," <^> mourned.

"< > have," < > said, for < > was still controlling the moves: </> had, being flawed, acquired two flawed entities, one flawed by nature, the other by invasion.

The important two were safe.

< > was awake again. All the way.

And the passengers scurried this way and that in panic, examining old alliances and likely advantage.

Only ((())) ranged the passages, wailing in ((())) 's madness. Perhaps only ((())) 's lower mind was left; perhaps some memory remained, what side ((())) had taken once. "Aaaaiiiieeeee," ((())) cried. "Help us, help us all! O strangers, rescue us!"

"Paul," Rafe said, who was not-Rafe, and something very strong.

Paul lay still and stared, heaving for breath in the all-enveloping dark while Rafe changed into something huge and slightly blurred. Paul flinched at this transformation and started to twist away, but Rafe's touch was gentle, very easy, on his shoulder.

"You're not him," Paul said, and his own voice seemed very distant in his ears, as if he had been drugged. Everything seemed far.

"You're safe," it told him, which he wanted now desperately to hear. "You're safe with me." The strangeness had gotten to the all-enveloping point and battered at his mind; and just when it was at its worst, it promised him safety and protection. He was ready to believe.

"I have you," the blurred shape said. The voice was Rafe's, but strange and deep, like a motor running. "You're very safe in my company. You don't have to worry while I'm here."

He let it hold him like a child. The voice sank to be one vast burr, that filled everything, replaced everything. It touched him, mother-gentle, spoke to him in a language eloquent of protection; and he shut his eyes, trusting finally, because he could only sustain the fear so long in such closeness, in an existence in which he could not tire or sleep: the voice went on and on.

"Let go," it hummed, "listen to me. You're safe."

"I'm dead," he said. "What's safe in that?"

"Not dead. Not truly. Not at all. You exist. You can come and go at will. You have long life ahead of you; and a comfortable one, with me. Be still, be quiet, rest. Nothing can reach you in my heart."

"We don't get hungry," Jillan said. "I could wish we got hungry. I miss—" She shook her head and stopped, wisely.

Rafe stared at her bleakly, remembering many things he missed. At length he got up and tried the barrier again. It still held and he came and sat down again, letting his shoulders fall. There was no pretending with Jillan. Finally they had passed all embarrassment, all other pretenses; he was naked inside and out with Rafe and stopped minding: now he could be that way with Jillan, at least in most things.

"Beats station life," he said, which was an old joke with them, that anything did. Even dying.

"Got ourselves a ship," she said, rising to it valiantly, but the grief never left her eyes. *Paul, Paul, Paul,* they said, wrath and divided loyalties.

"Got ourselves a big one," he said.

"What we have to do," she said, "we find our way to controls—in our android shapes—and then we *take* this thing."

"Deal," he said.

But they sat there, with a barrier about them. With Paul missing, and neither of them made guesses about Paul.

He'll find a way to rescue us, Rafe thought, trying to convince himself. *He's still loose, he's smart—So's Rafe—*without modesty. *But Paul can move through the ship. . . .*

Maybe it's taking Paul apart now.

"Idea," said Jillan.

"What?"

"Rafe. They're keeping Rafe locked up. That means he could do damage."

"They're keeping us locked up too," he said, and they turned that thought over separately for a moment.

"Huh," she said, his Ma'am; his number One, his crew.

"I'll make you a present of this ship," he said.

"That's the Old Man talking," she said, seeming to take heart. "You do that, Rafe. Let's find something to break, when we get out of here."

"No way," he said. "It's our ship, remember. We want this thing intact."

The chittering came back, the wailing thing passed, as it had passed before. He refused to wince, refused even to acknowledge it.

When we get out of here.

Then, in a blink, Paul was lying a dozen feet beyond them.

Jillan moved, scrambled to Paul's side with a soft, frightened oath.

Rafe moved up and knelt again, cautious of such gifts. "Paul," he said.

Paul opened his eyes to pale slits, shuddered and came suddenly wide-eyed, lurching up on his arm.

"Where are we?" Paul asked. "O God, where are we? Jillan—?" He sat upright, looked down at his own body, at theirs—panicked, darting glances. *"What is this place?"*

"The same as it's ever been," Rafe said.

"What do you mean, the same?" Paul's voice rode close to breaking. "Where are we? Where's the ship?"

"He doesn't remember," Rafe said, at Jillan's frightened glance his way. "He's lost it all."

"Lost what?" asked Paul. *"What* don't I remember?"

Rafe put out a hand and held it on his shoulder. "This place— you've lost a little time, Paul. Just take it easy. We're all right. Take it easy. We'll fill you in."

Paul was scared again, mortally scared. So was Jillan; he could read it in that thin-lipped calm.

"It's all right," Jillan said. "It's all right, we've got you back. We lost you for a while. You scared us, Paul."

< > listened for a time. < > had debated with < >self, how much interference was wise, whether to restore Paul to the set at all. And then it occurred to < > that a different waking experience might change the Paul-mind to some advantage.

So < > had restored him to the others, this copy fresh from its death experience.

</> would know that, of course. There remained the very strong likelihood </> would attempt a substitution the moment </> had a chance.

But < > took the risk. Perhaps Jillan or Rafe-mind had left its influence on < >. < > was not sure. Many entities had tried; but their desire to keep that set intact was strong.

There was also, native to < >self and them—curiosity.

< > took up the Rafe-image again and visited the corridor, finding Rafe asleep.

< > squatted there, just watching, running through the feelings Rafe-mind had about himself and his living original. Then:

"Wake up," Rafe heard. "Wake up, Rafe."

He opened his eyes, knowing the voice, braced himself back on his hands in a scramble for the wall, for it was close, until he had gotten his thoughts together.

"Which one are you?"

His own face smiled back at him, answering that question. Rafe Two would have been puzzled at the least.

"Stay back," Rafe said.

"You know I can't touch you."

He let go his breath, still pressed as close against the wall as he could get. "Like hell. You promised me the others back. Where are they?"

"Plotting together. They want to take the ship."

"Good for them."

The alien grinned, squatted there with his elbows on naked knees, went sober once again. "It's not too likely a threat."

"I want to see them."

"Ship's important to you, isn't it? I think about this star where I found you; this mind doesn't care. I think of others. But when I think of *ship,* it reacts. Like love. Like need. It feels strong as sex-drive. Stronger, maybe. But *Lindy*'s finished, I'm afraid. It was, you'll pardon me, not much of a ship to start with."

"Shut up."

"On the other hand," the doppelganger said, "—I love that idea, you know? The other hand. I understand a number of things: you'd want to be dropped as far away from Endeavor as you could get. They'd ask questions there at Endeavor, years of questions. There and at Cyteen. I could drop you, oh, say, Paradise. There'd be questions there, too; but maybe less anxiety. Less chance of your being—confined. Wouldn't you say?"

He sat and listened to this prattle, roused out of sleep to listen, tucked up against the wall. He ignored most of it, let it drift through his mind and out again, refusing to let it stick. "Stop playing this game. I don't care where you drop me."

"I want to prepare a canister for you. This takes a little time. I won't stay long at all at Paradise, not to make a stir."

"What's your name?"

"My name?"

"You've got a name of your own the way I presume you've got a shape. What is it?"

It seemed to think a moment. "Kepta, if you like."

"Kepta. What are you really up to?"

"Right now," the doppelganger said, "I'm merely clearing decks. I'll take another impression before I turn you out; this will put me up to date with all you've gotten here. I've put that off; it is stressful. But that's the only thing I want of you."

"The others. What will happen to them?"

"I won't turn them off, if that's what you mean. That's the last thing I'd do."

"Meaning what?"

"They're mine," Kepta said.

"What do you mean, yours? You mean you're taking them somewhere?"

"They can hardly leave the ship with you—can they? No, there's nothing really to worry about at all. I could put some of this business off; but on the other hand—I'd like to get you to the lab, just to make sure, well, of having that copy. It's my only condition." The image got to its feet, held out a hand. "Come on, get up. I'd like you to walk there."

"Meaning there are other choices?"

"There are other ways."

Rafe thought that over, staring up into his own face, hating the mock-regretful look on it. He put his hands on the gossamer-carpeted floor and shoved himself up, straightened and glared at the image eye to eye, but it refused the confrontation, walked off a way and held out its hand, beckoning.

"Come on."

"Why should I believe this, when you haven't come through with the other promise? I want to see the others, hear?"

"Afterward. I promise. Come on, now, Rafe. Let's not be difficult."

"Let's," he echoed sourly. "What *is* my choice?"

"I really don't want to do that."

"What?"

"I could send something in here to bring you. I'd have it carry you and spare you the long walk; but walking makes it your choice, that's why I want you to do it. I really think that's valuable."

"You know, I never noticed it; I don't like the way I talk."

"Humor?"

Rafe said nothing, but started walking; looked back again, at home, at *Lindy*'s jumbled fragments, then fell in beside Kepta's light-dim shape. "I need anything?"

"No. Not really."

He walked farther; the image walked, with smooth efficiency: *sequencing projectors,* he had decided once. *Projected from what? Fibers in the rug?* "This going to hurt much?" he asked finally.

"Yes," Kepta said.

They walked along, down the snaking corridor of gossamer-green humps and hillocks. The lights were all on, showing him the way.

"Haven't felt any push on this ship," he said. "We're inertial, aren't we?"

"Some ways off Endeavor, plus one plus thirty plus ten, one-tenth C. Make you feel better, knowing where you are?"

He nodded, relationships and directions flashing into shape. He felt familiar stars about him again. Home space. He drew a shuddering, long breath, pretended nonchalance. "Big nothing out here."

"It's a vacant spot. Where we're not disturbed."

Chapter Six

They walked side by side, he and Kepta, into that vast empty node where many halls converged—silent: his footfalls on the padded floor made no great sound. Rafe heard only the whisper of his clothing, his own deepened breaths. Kepta made no sound at all, except to talk to him from time to time down the winding hall:

"Tired?" Kepta asked.

"Does that matter? You pushed me along this way once, with the lights. What were you after, then?"

"Reactions," Kepta said.

He strode on a few more limping steps. "Like now?"

A few steps more. "No," Kepta said. "Now I know exactly what you'll do."

He looked at Kepta, but Kepta did not, seemingly, look his way.

"You're limited," Rafe asked him, the question flashing to his mind, "to one vantage point? To that shape? Those eyes?"

"No," Kepta said again.

"Physically—where are you?"

Silence.

"Makes you nervous? You scared, are you, to answer that?"

Silence still.

They came into the dark, warted heart of the huge meeting of corridors. Light came from home-corridor at their backs, a soft glow that lit the whole floor ahead in a dim gray succession of ripples and hummocks, stalagmites and lumpish stalactites afflicted with gossamer-shrouded warts and protuberances. There were no echoes. No sound. The carpet drank it up. "Can't afford lights here?" Rafe jibed at Kepta, trying to learn, by whatever questions Kepta would answer. "You don't like light, that it? Or don't you need it?"

Lights flared, illuminating a vast chamber, a craziness of lumps and hummocks and tunnels on a mammoth scale; lights died and left him in dark again, as suddenly.

Kepta was gone.

"Kepta?" He faced wildly about, flash-blinded, helpless, stumbling on the uneven floor. *"Kepta?"*

"First passage on your left," a voice said, close by him. The gold-glowing image resumed. "Just checking. I'm a little narrow-focused in this shape; a great deal of me is doing other things, and now and again I like to take a little look behind the eyes, so to say. That's right, this way. Not far now."

His heart pounded. He rubbed at his eyes trying to get his vision back, stumbling on the uneven floor, staying with Kepta in a winding course around the prominences. They skirted around a jutting protuberance of the wall and passed one black corridor opening. The next acquired dim light, showing gray and green no different than otherwhere.

"This way," Kepta said.

He matched Kepta's drifting pace. The way narrowed into a twisting gut, went from gossamer-green to bald glistening plastic in a green that deepened to livid unpleasantness.

Narrower still, and brighter-lit. "O God," Rafe said, and balked. Metal gleamed. Clusters of projections like insect limbs lined the chamber which unfurled from beyond the turning—some arms folded, some thrust out in partial extension, things to grip and bite, extensors armed with knives.

"Come on," Kepta said. "Come ahead. That's right. No sense running now."

"It's still there," Rafe Two said. They had tried the unseen barrier now and again, when one and the other of them grew restless in their dark confinement. He went back and sat down while Jillan and Paul had their own go at it, Paul with violence, which did no good, but it satisfied some need, and Rafe averted his face and rested his chin on his arm, knee tucked up, staring into the dark beyond the invisible wall.

Now and again there were sounds. The thing that wailed had become familiar, still dreadful when it came, but it seemed by now that it would have done something, attacked if it could or if it had the desire.

"Shut up," he told it when it came.

Paul and Jillan sat down again, Paul last, who cast himself down and hung his hands between his knees, to look up again with a bleak, sullen stare.

He was being patient, was Paul, amnesiac, wiped of everything recent, even the remembrance that he was dead. They had had to tell him that all over again, and Paul had sat and listened, and objected. Perhaps he thought they were crazy; perhaps he believed it. Whatever Paul believed, he was quiet about it all.

Because Jillan was calm, Rafe thought; because he and Jillan accepted it and explained matters gently as they could. He detected the cracks in Paul's facade, the little signs of tension, the occasional sharp answer, the increasingly worried look on Paul's face when they failed to retaliate for his gibes. They were shielding him; Paul realized it. Jillan protected him—being merchanter-born, tough in spacer-ways, with a spacer's tolerance of distances, infinities, time and thinking inside-out. She was the stronger here. So was he.

Jillan and me, Rafe thought, *and Paul, on the other side, cut off from her. From me. He's trying—so hard to keep himself together in Jillan's sight, up to her measure of a man—We joke; we seem to take it light; it's like salt in all his wounds.*

He got up, paced, for Paul's sake, to be human. Pushed at the wall.

"Give it up," Paul said.

He sat down again, slumped, elbows on knees.

So maybe it helped, giving Paul a way to seem calm and in control.

"Got any ideas?" he asked Paul then.

Paul was silent a long time. "Just thinking," Paul said, "that we don't eat, don't sleep, don't get tired—wonder how long it takes a mind to unravel, sitting still. Wonder if it's listening. Or if it's just gone off and forgotten us, this alien you met. Wonder if we're all crazy. Or you are. And we sit here glowing in the dark."

Rafe laughed. It was conscious effort. He remembered—a thing that turned him cold; a meeting Jillan had not known; that Paul assuredly had not; and for a moment he was the one pretending cheerfulness. It had hurt; it would happen again, he thought, for no reason, for nothing that made sense.

"Sooner or later," he began dutifully to answer Paul; but something caught his eye, a light far out in the dark.

"Something's out there," Jillan said, scrambling to her feet as he did. "Something's coming—"

It moved in that rapid way things could here. Paul got to his feet and Jillan held to him, steadying him by that contact.

It whipped up to the barrier, a human runner.

Paul.

Doppelganger's doppelganger. It stared, stark and wide-mouthed, glowing like themselves, and with one strangled cry of grief, it spun and ran away, diminished as rapidly as it had come.

"What was *that?*" asked Paul, remarkably calm, considering the horror in his eyes.

Rafe turned and looked at him, far from calm himself—considered this second Paul-shape that had materialized inside the barrier with him and Jillan.

Jillan too, he remembered—the arms that had gripped him with more than human strength—

He set his back to the phantom wall, facing both of them, their united, guarded stare.

The pain—O God, the pain!

Rafe screamed while he had breath, while he had the strength. But it was too deep and too long, too thorough, pinned him between breaths and held him dying there until air began the long slow leak back into his lungs. Then the cycle ran round again.

And over again.

"There," said Kepta's vast slow voice after all eternity. "There. That's over now." And there was dark a time.

"Try to move," it said.

Rafe moved; he would have done anything it told him, not to have the pain. He kept moving and thrust aching arms under him, took the strain of muscle-stretch across his aching ribs, his belly, trying constantly to find some position that did not hurt and discovering fresh agonies at every shift.

"Easy," Kepta said out of that vast haze of his senses, awareness of light, machines that hummed and moved, having him as a mote in their cold heart. A metal arm moved at his face, thrust a tube into his mouth with persistent accuracy, shot a dose of tepid water down his throat. Other arms moved spiderlike about him and closed about his arms, *click-click*. He was past all but the vaguest fear. He let his limbs be moved because gentle as it was he had resisted once and found no limit to its strength. *Click-click*. It faced him about and held him upright as he sat on the table.

"Over, then?" His voice was a ragged croak, his throat raw from screaming. "Over?"

"All done," Kepta said, taking shape in front of him. "Rest a bit."

He was willing; the spider arms stayed still, like a cradle behind him. He leaned his head back, his feet dangling off the edge of the machinery. For a moment he blurred out again, head resting against the arms, heart still laboring, while the tears leaked from his eyes and the sweat slicked his skin.

"Where is it?" he asked then, meaning the thing that he had birthed. He had some proprietary curiosity; it had cost him so much pain.

"Here," Kepta said, "here in the machine."

"You mean you'll give it a body."

"No," Kepta said, and rested a ghostly hand on a large hummock that rose with several others to form the table, the base of several of the arms. "It has one. In here. Do you want to know how it works? Your template of a moment ago exists now. It will never know more than you knew when it was made. Always when I call it up it will be at the same moment."

Rafe shook his head and shut his eyes, feeling everything slide into chaos, not wanting this.

"So I can always recover that point," Kepta said, "at need. A point of knowledge—and ignorance."

Eyes slitted, till Kepta was a golden blur: "You still going to let me go?"

"Oh, yes." Kepta moved among the machinery, through one lowered metal arm. "You asked about bodies. This one—" Kepta laid a hand on his own insubstantial chest. "You assume there's some substance to it, somewhere. There's not. It's a pattern. You want Jillan? I can call up that template. Or Paul. Or one of several of you."

Paul One ran, raced into the dark, sobbing at what he had seen: himself; himself possessing Jillan and Rafe and he-himself watching helplessly from outside—

At last he found Rafe again, his own Rafe, beaconlike in the nowhereland, that shape that was Rafe and not, something blurred and larger, far larger.

"I know what you found," Rafe said. "I knew you would." And Rafe himself blurred further, into outlines vast and dark. "I knew it would hurt. Paul—"

"Was it me?" he asked. "Was that my real body?"

"No," it said. "Only another duplicate."

There was no more system of reference, nothing human left. It took him in its changing arms, took him to its heart, whispered to him in a voice still human though the rest of it was not.

"You don't have to be afraid. I won't hurt you, nothing will ever hurt you while I have you. You can't trust what you see, that's the first thing you have to learn. You want to be safe. But I can make you strong. You won't be afraid of anything. You want to know how this ship works? I'll tell you. Anything you want to know. That version you just saw? Nothing. Nothing. Another copy off your template. I have to tell you how that works, that next. The templates."

"I recorded you," Kepta said, waving a hand past the mounded protrusions beneath all the array of shining spider arms, "not just the outward form, but at every level, in every function and structure— everything. The template's as like you as if you'd been spun out in bits, down to the state and spin of your particles: that's how exact it is . . . all uncertainties made definite, particulate memory, frozen in the finest definition matter can achieve. We just—play it out again. Call it up in memory and let it integrate. The visible manifestation, the body—a very simple thing: just light, quite apart from the more complex patterns. An image conceived off the template and maintained by quite inelegant means: the computer knows its shape, that's all, and revises it moment by moment by the direction of the program; but that program that animates it—that's quite another thing."

"It reacts," Rafe said. "It *thinks*—"

"That's the elegance. It does."

"You've turned them to machines."

"No. Contained them in one. They react; they think; they think they move. They're programs, if you like, smart programs that can learn and change, that get input they interpret in the same way they always did, or they think they do, that eyes work and mouths make speech, and muscles move. The body—is merely light, for passing convenience. It changes in response to signals the programs give. It can't input. But on other levels, in the purest sense, the programs can input from each other, can imagine, tend to perceive what they expect —like smells and textures. Illusions, if you like. But they aren't. The programs aren't. They grow, and change, get experience, change their minds. They stay up and running until someone shuts them down."

Rafe shook his head. The words writhed past, heard, half-heard. He hung there in the spider arms, looked at the machines, the mocking image of himself. "One large memory," he said past unresponsive lips, "one hell of a large memory, that thing. Wouldn't it be?"

"Oh yes, quite large."

"Runs all the time."

Kepta lifted his head in a curious way, his own mannerism thrown back at him, half-mocking, half-wary.

"I threaten you," Rafe said, and found it funny, hanging there, naked, in the steel, unyielding hands. "Do I? Suppose I believe that's how you do it, suppose I believe it all—There's still the why of it. You want to tell me why? And you still want to tell me you're putting me out of here?"

"Why's not relevant. Say that I wanted the template. That's all. When I call it up and it talks to me, it won't know a thing of what we've said; won't know what it is. It'll be the you that walked in here of his own free will. That's the one I'll deal with. Why tell you anything? The template won't remember. You'd have to tell it what you've learned. And you'll be safe away from it."

"Why?" he asked again. "Why let me go?"

"I said. It's easy.—You're worried, aren't you? You're worried about your life, theirs—the whole species. That's why you don't really think I'll turn you out. You think of ships. Military. I understand this concept of yours, this collective of self defense. You think I've come to learn all I can; that I'm in advance of others who'll come to harm all your kind. No. I'm unique."

"Then come in. Come into some human port and talk like you're civilized."

The mirror-image blinked. "You don't really want that."

"No," he said, thinking again, thinking at once of Endeavor, magnified a hundred-fold, *O God, some major port—*

"There'll just be yourself returning," it said. "The military will check records, put you together with the Endeavor business. You'll be answering a lot of questions. That's all right. Tell them anything you like. I'll be long gone from Paradise."

"Where? To do what?"

"You're worrying again."

"Are you afraid? Afraid of us?"

"*Responsibility.* You have this tendency—to make yourself the center, the focus. Jillan and Paul—you're responsible for them; if your species died, you'd be more *responsible* than I who killed them. An interesting concept, responsibility—and within your context, yes, you could become that focus. I could wipe out your kind, based on what you know. And on what you don't. You couldn't fight me. Your ships can't catch me; my weapons are beyond you; there's just no chance, if I were interested. I'm not. So you're not the center, are you? That's a great loss to you . . . that your kind will live on without your responsibility. Could it even be—that you're not responsible for other things? Or that your friends are not in your universe at all?"

"What becomes of them?"

"They're not your responsibility."

He flung himself for his feet. The arms prevented that.

"You're not necessary. You go to Paradise. You tell them what you like. Tell them everything you've seen. They'll be interested. Of course they will. You'll be famous of your kind—in certain ways. Very important. You'll certainly be the focus then. Won't you?"

Imagination filled it in—official disclaimers, the military swarming over him and his capsule like bees—*Hallucination,* they'd say, for general consumption. . . . "Damn you," he said to Kepta, shivering.

"Not my responsibility," Kepta said. "Not at all. I'll be gone. Nothing to fear from me; there never was. But you don't want to believe that. It takes something away from you." The spider-arms relaxed, the grip yielded. "Your clothes are there. I think you might be cold."

He moved, on his own, crawled off the sweating, plastic surface. Everywhere about him was the stench of his own fear. He tucked his clothing to him and held onto it. "I stink," he muttered at it. "I want a bath. I'm going back to *Lindy,* thanks."

Kepta would stop him, he thought; would move the arms again. But they all retracted with one massive snick of metal, clearing him a path.

"A machine could carry you," Kepta said.

"I'll walk."

It hurt. Every movement hurt, however slow. Every thought did, in this trap that he was in. He limped toward the exit from this place, the way he had come in. He cherished the pain, that it filled his mind like needful ballast, filled cracks and crevices and darknesses and took away the need to think. Tears ran down his face, and he could not have said whether they were true tears or only a welling up of too much fluid; he was beyond all analyses.

< > destroyed the Rafe-simulacrum that < > wore and expanded past its limits with relief. < > had already absorbed everything that surfaced in Rafe-mind, all the suppositions, all the facts, all the emotive feeling. < > felt a lingering distress.

There was a time of adjustment afterward, there must be, in which < >'s human experiences and < >'s own flowed past each other in comparison, and < > kept them all. < > was interested for various reasons, but one reason assumed priority, that < > was due for challenge—indeed, had, to a great extent provoked it, seeing opportunity. More, there was additional use in Rafe-mind—for < /> had worn it. Ancient and unbending as < /> was, < /> had slipped into it, and this was worth interest. It was always well, under any circumstances, to know just what $</>$ was about.

And if $</>$ had found some congruency to $</>$self in Rafemind, then $<>$ was interested.

"Is it pleasant?" $<>$ taunted $</>$ across the width of the ship.

$</>$ had no answer, $</>$ had taken a shape much more like $</>$'s own configurations, and the Paul-mind nested in it.

$<>$ was thunderstruck.

"See," said $<^>$ in an undertone of distress as $<^>$ came slipping up to $<>$'s presence. "See, $<^>$ said as much. So did ((())). Even ((()))."

"Quiet," said $<>$, losing all amusement, and having searched the tag ends of Rafe-mind to account for the disaster, decided finally that Paul Gaines was, in this simulacrum, more than slightly warped.

Paul-mind, Rafe-mind informed $<>$, was *stationer,* and that meant a wealth of things. It meant a life style; it meant groups; and security; and comfort if one could get the value-items to exchange for it—which was one motivation for human ships moving constantly in transfer of materials from collection to consumption (but not the sole motive of those who *ran* those ships). This thread led to comprehensions. Paul-mind was not like Rafe. Paul Gaines wanted to be contained in something, in anything. Space frightened him; strangeness did; but what provided him comfort was never strange to Paul.

And there Paul sat, in $</>$'s heart, nested, protected and surviving.

$<>$ was, to admit it, utterly chagrined.

Paul has other qualities, the Rafe-memories said. Rafe-mind called it bravery, and attached whole complexes of valuations to that word. Not group-survival over individual, though that was part of it. Not retaliation simply, though it might manifest in that; or equally well, by its negative. Not self-aggrandizement, either, though it could be that; or equally well self-denial. The term attached to valuations of person —the affirmation of some ideal species-type, $<>$ judged.

Rafe-mind was not sure it itself possessed this quality; but it desired it. To evidence that it did possess it, Rafe tried not to be disturbed.

For that reason Rafe had walked the corridor to the lab, while paradoxically the remnant of Rafe-mind $<>$ still retained, recognized this act for what it was, that Rafe might comply and intend at the same time to make violent resistance, the moment Rafe had the chance.

Rafe-mind called this second concept dignity.

< > thought of it as self-preservation, but remembered it was, per-haps, strategy as well, that Rafe did this thing for all the group he perceived as his.

Responsibility.

And what group does Paul belong to? < > wondered, having infor-mation about the words Old Man, and ship, and an arrangement < > found disturbingly accusatory.

< > was Old Man too; < > had such a group. They were the passengers. Responsibility, Rafe would say again. < > felt no such thing. But to be the focus of loyalty, that appealed to < >.

< / > would appropriate this Paul Gaines. There was no likelihood that < / > would not, having no such thing as loyalty < / >self.

Easier, < > thought, if Paul had met some segment of = = = =. Desire for containment, indeed. The Cannibal could have provided that, had < > not intervened.

"Mad," said <ᴧ>, nesting close to < >, which < > sometimes permitted. "Pity him, < >."

"Paul would find <ᴧ> quite disturbing," < > said. "So would all of them."

"<ᴧ> know that," <ᴧ> said. And, extraneously, as <ᴧ> often spoke: "<ᴧ> know bravery."

<ᴧ> had a certain skill, to dip into < >'s mind without leaving anything behind, not a unique talent, by any means. It was < >'s nature, and the ship's. "It is not——" < > said, and named a concept in <ᴧ>'s terms.

"It feels like that," <ᴧ> said. "<ᴧ> would have walked down that hall."

"Of course <ᴧ> would," < > said, unsurprised. "For somewhat skewed reasons. It is not——" and < > named that word again, which neither Rafe-mind nor Jillan-mind (which < > also had) pos-sessed the biological reflexes to understand.

"Go," < > said to <ᴧ>, "and tell < / > that < / > need not skulk about. It's merely < / >'s paranoid suppositions that < > would in-terfere."

"</> supposes that < > can't," <ᴧ> said. "</> said to tell < > so."

< > sent a pulse through the ship, violent enough to touch any sense. "So much for can't," < > said, and went off to keep a thing for which the Rafe-mind had no complete word, but *promise* was close enough.

Rafe Two sat, tucked up against the dark, invisible wall; and Jillan and Paul kept to their side of the containment. They stared at one another. That was all that was left to do in the limbo they were in.

"I have to explain," Rafe had said, taking that position from some time ago, "what happened to me." He spoke quite calmly, quite rationally, thinking of his back against an interface that something might pierce very unexpectedly; his face toward—"I'm not sure what you are," he had said to them. "That Paul that came up to us, that's not the only double that exists. There was you too—Jillan. It got me. Strong, really strong. It took me to that place, that—" He did not like to remember it. "I don't know what it did; it hurt. Like the first time. Maybe it did some adjustment. Maybe—maybe it did something else." Suppositions about that had tormented him thus far; he did not fully trust himself. "I'm telling all of it, you see. I just don't know what it did to me. But it used you to get at me. Now I don't know what I'm locked up with. Just let's keep to our own sides of this place awhile."

There had been pain on Jillan's face. That was the worst.

"Well," she had said in a quiet tone, "I can pretty well guess it's you. That's something. And I can tell you it's me, but I guess you won't believe that."

"I'm not one of them," Paul had said next, and shifted uncomfortably, arms about his knees, while both of them looked at him. "I can swear to you I'm not. There was—there was, remember, this bar on Fargone where we used to meet. The man there had this bird, remember, this live bird—"

"Named Mickey," Jillan said.

"Lived on frozen fruit," Rafe had said himself, remembering the creature, the curiosity, the small reminder there were worlds, that Earth was real somewhere.

—Their captors would be interested in that; homeworld; center of origin. A chill went up Rafe's unprotected back.

"There's one double of you," he had said to Paul. "Maybe more of us. But just stay there. On your side. Please."

"He was a pretty thing," Jillan said at last, "that bird."

"He bit," Paul said.

"Don't blame him," Jillan said. "I'd bite too, being stared at." She hunched her shoulders, looked around, dropped the subject altogether.

"Wish I had a beer," Rafe said.

"Downer wine," said Paul. "You know I bet it got that last bottle."

"Couldn't have come through that spin."

"Bet it did. Bet Rafe's got it. They gave him everything."

"Can't share with him," Rafe said, playing the small game, talk-talk, anything to fill the silence; but he mourned the wine he could never touch.

Paul frowned, who had never seen what they described to him, the place where they walked through furniture and walls or his living self's offered hands.

And Paul's disbelief comforted him, one small confirmation that seemed least likely to be contrived.

But maybe it's smart enough to do that, Rafe thought, growing paranoid. *Maybe it's got all the twitches down.*

He did not know the alien's limits, that was all. He stared at his sister and his friend and could not believe in either of them.

And abruptly they were gone.

He leapt up.

In light, in a tunneled hall of nodes and gossamer-on carpet.

His living self lay there on the floor, in a nest of blankets and disordered clothes.

"Rafe," he said.

There was no response. The living body looked sorrowfully small, tight-curled among the blankets. He walked over and squatted down, immune to heat and cold himself, put out a hand—living habits were hard to break—to the sleeper's shoulder. "Rafe," he said, with great tenderness, because somehow, somewhen, and not because they were identical, he had come to love his other self, to think of him as brother, and to have a little pride in himself—without modesty—because of this steady, loyal man. "Rafe, wake up. Come on. Come out of it."

The sleeper moved and groaned in pain.

It was a doppelganger—one of them at least. Rafe stared at it leaning above him with the light shining through its body, then struggled to sit up and heave his naked back against the wall.

"What do you want?" he said, in what of a voice the hoarseness left.

"You're hurt. It hurt you."

"Some." Rafe shut his eyes. The light wanted to fuzz. He opened them again, discontent, for the ceiling light interfered and blurred out part of the doppelganger's form. They were only holograms, the alien had said. And other things he clamped his jaws upon.

The manner was not Kepta, he thought. Or it was Kepta playing still more bitter jokes, with that anguished, frightened look.

"I'm all right," he said to it, to him. "Just a little sore."

"What in God's name did it want? What did it do to you?"

"Just a look-over. A workout. I don't know. It hurt. That was incidental, I think it was. How are you?"

The doppelganger laughed, not a pleasant, happy laugh, but one of irony, all the answer it gave him.

"How's Jillan and Paul?" he asked it then. "Paul still not speaking to me?"

A shadow touched the eyes. "Paul's better now."

Better now. He drew an uneasy breath. *Which one are you?* "I really wish," he said, "you'd back off a bit. The light is in my eyes."

The doppelganger reached; he flinched, twitched back. "You're scared," it said. "Scared of me."

"Who are you?"

"Me. Rafe. It's used my shape with you. Has it?"

"Yes. It has. *Our* shape, friend. You know about that?"

"What did it do?"

"Its name is Kepta. He or she. I don't know." Rafe's voice cracked. "Maybe you could say."

The doppelganger shook its head solemnly, its eyes locked on his own. "It got me too. It used Jillan's shape. I've seen something using Paul's. And it hurt."

"It copied you." It made sense then, in a tangled skein of threads.

"That was copy-making, friend. Now it's got three versions of me and you. Four, counting the original."

"Me; the one it made from me; you—"

"It got me," Rafe said. "That's how I know. Mine's four. I saw the machines—" The voice cracked again. His joints felt racked. "Plays havoc with the nerves. Goes all through your body. Copies everything."

"Why? For God's sake, what's it doing with us?"

"It wants different versions. You've grown." He thought now he knew which one it was; there was no way to be sure, only to guess. He guessed. "You're not me, not the way you were; I'm not that me either. It just took a new impression. That's all. It's going to let me go, it says."

"Let you go. Where?"

"Says Paradise."

"How'd it know that? How much does it know?"

"Like names and places?" He stared into the doppelganger's face, and thoughts came to him, knowing this self, its need to know—

—its own condition. To know what it was. The doppelganger had no idea, he suspected; no idea at all what he really was, or where.

"It's got access to everything," Rafe told it carefully. "It has my mannerisms; yours; my turns of speech; everything I know. Like names. It wants to know a star the way we name it. It's got a map in my head; it just overlays that on the charts it knows. So it knows Paradise, Fargone, knows everything—"

"Mickey."

"What Mickey?"

"The bird in that Fargone bar."

"I guess it does. I'd forgotten. I guess it could remember. Probably has better recall than I do."

"Jillan remembers it, really well."

"Meaning it's got us all."

"I don't know," the doppelganger said, hugging himself round the knees. "I don't *know*. What's it up to? You figure that?"

"It says it doesn't matter. Kepta. Kepta's what it calls itself. It says —" His voice gave way again. "—says it's got no military aims. That it could take our *species* out. The whole human race. Says it's not interested."

The doppelganger stared at him.

"I think," Rafe said, "maybe it could, near enough as wouldn't matter. Its tech is—way ahead. Got circuits, memory storage, stuff I can get around; it's mechanical, like that. But the power it throws around, the way its computers work—" He shut his eyes while he swallowed; it hurt. "I don't know comp's insides; you know that; we just run the things. But this ship's got tricks we don't. That's a fact. Doesn't even hurt to say. It runs through our heads all it likes, digs up everything it wants. Think of trying to defend our space from one of *us* who'd just inherited this whole ship and aimed it at humankind. If we wanted to—we could be real trouble, given what this has. And it is trouble. Knows every target. Every ship." He blinked. Tears spilled, a wetness at outer edge of his right eye. "Amazing what's not classified. Can't be, can it? Where worlds and stations are—any human knows the star names, and God help us, we know the charts. Any human knows how to run machines; so it knows what we've got. And what we don't have. That too."

"How many of it are there?"

"That's a real good question, isn't it? It says *I*. That's all I know."

"Easier if it were."

"Easier to *what?* Fight this thing?".

"Got nothing better to do," the doppelganger said. "Maybe it's going to do everything it said, let you go, just go its way and let human space alone. If it does, that's fine. If it doesn't—well, we're still here, aren't we? We'll fix it."

"It can shut you down."

"So," the doppelganger said with a small, worried shrug. "There's several of us, aren't there?"

"One of us—" Rafe felt a new and spreading chill. *"Rafe, there's five of us."*

"How, five?"

"Versions. Me. One before I waked. That made you, but *it* still exists. Naïve as it ever was. There's you; that's three. There's the version of you it just got. Four. There's the me it recorded, the stupid one that walked into that lab and lay down where it said, and let itself be recorded because it had no way to know—"

"No way to stop it either."

"But that's five. You see what the difference is. Mindsets. Number one's straight out of the wreck, shaken up and scared; two's me, who's been through everything; three's you,—we're oldest, seen the most. Four's you without this meeting; five's me who was willing to lie down in that machine and hoped I'd get out—It can take any branch of us it likes. Live in it. Watch it work. Twist it any way it likes."

"You mean it's not just a mask it wears," the doppelganger said, his brow knit up in worry, in far too little worry.

Rafe stared at him. *Tell him?* he wondered. *Tell him what he is?* He knew his own limits, how much truth he could bear. *Sorry, brother, you're repeatable. Jillan, Paul, them too.*

"Maybe it'll really let you go," the doppelganger said at last. "I hope it does."

"You're lying," Rafe said. "You need me."

The doppelganger shook his head. "No. I want you out of here. With all the rest that means. That it's not interested in us. That it *won't* attack."

"And what becomes of you, then? You don't die, man. You can't. What happens to you?" He wished at once he had never said it. He saw the fear it caused, the sudden freezing of mirror-Rafe's expression.

The doppelganger shrugged then. "That is a problem, isn't it?" He dropped down to sit flat against the floor, against the illusion of it—

—*because he expects a floor,* Rafe thought.

"But it's our problem," the doppelganger said. "Not yours. For one thing you can't very well tell it no. For another—let's just get you out of here, if we can. You can get hurt. Call it sympathy pains, if you like. Self-preservation. Something of the sort. Just take our surviving substance out of here, first chance you get. What's it going to do, walk into Paradise Station with you?"

"Capsule with a beeper."

The doppelganger frowned. "Chancy."

"Scares me too. But it was the best you could think of."

"Don't make jokes like that."

"Sorry. But it's true."

The doppelganger slumped, arms against his knees. "At least it's not going inside Paradise," he said.

"At least. There's that to be grateful for." He leaned back against the wall, tucked the blanket up about his arms. "You don't think you can trust Jillan—or Paul."

"I don't know which copy I'm dealing with," the doppelganger said in desperation. "It sent me here. Without warning. Rafe, it's got them both."

Chapter Seven

There was no one. Where Paul had been in their confinement, was suddenly no one, in the time it took to blink, the way it had taken Rafe; and Jillan Murray lurched to her feet all in one wild motion, stifling the outcry—*no good, no good to yell.* The dark was absolute, featureless, soundless; she stood sense-deprived and still, bereft of everyone.

"Jillan," said a female voice. Her own doppelganger blinked into green-gold glow in front of her, naked flesh a little bony about the ribs.

"That you?" she said, all cold. "That you, self?"

"No," her own voice came back to her, from mirror-image lips.

Her knees wanted to shake. If she tried to run they would fail. *"My turn, is it?"*

It stood still, with a pensive, frowning look which slowly changed as if thought were going on behind the eyes and arrived at puzzlement. "It feels as if," it said, "you get some satisfaction from my coming round to you."

"Huh." She laughed.

"Very bitter satisfaction. You were really afraid—of being discounted in favor of the men in this situation. It's a very confused feeling."

Her skin felt like sweat she could not shed. *This is crazy,* she thought. *Should I run?*

Strong, Rafe had said. And: *It got me. Got me*—in ways unspecified.

"Anger," the doppelganger said, "that comes through."

"That doesn't take mind-reading. Where am I? Where are we? Dammit, *why?*"

The doppelganger's head came up a bit, a centering of the eyes, her eyes, beneath an untidy fringe of bangs.

"Take a walk with me."

"Like hell."

It blinked. "You did ask for answers."

"You can tell me what I asked. Right here."

And Paul was there, behind the doppelganger, lying still and helpless on the dark immaterial floor. He vanished as quickly. "Creation and uncreation," the doppelganger said. "That's what you are. No more, no less."

She was shaking. Pockets, she thought extraneously, wanting somewhere to put her hands; her hands missed pockets, touched only naked skin. "So, well," she said, "is that trick supposed to mean something?"

"Not in terms you're used to thinking of. Life and death are valueless. You're here. Your body's long since gone. But you're still living. So was that. Now it's gone. Want it back again?"

It was. It vanished.

"Dead again," it said. "Or gone. However you define it."

She swung at the doppelganger.

She was on the floor, loose-jointed, with the memory of blinding pain, sound, shock that ached in the roots of her teeth; and it stood just out of reach. It squatted down, arms on knees.

"Doesn't it occur to you," it said, "that I could just turn you off?"

Jillan got an elbow under her amid her shivering, pushed up, sat, as far as half squared her with its eyes. She glared at it, and nothing occurred to her, nothing in clear focus, but a dim, small fear that if she hit it again she would get the same hard shock. She had done no damage to it. None.

It sat there, a long, long moment. "Your mind's different," it said.

"Self-preservation . . . differently defined. I've seen you through Rafe's eyes. Your mind is shocked at his simplicity. So is Rafe-mind, to know you so thoroughly. Devastated."

"Shut up!"

"That's your strength," it said, this double of herself, this thing with shaggy, disordered hair and infinity in its eyes. "Rafe-mind wouldn't have attacked me bare-handed for anything but one of you. He's afraid to die. So are you. But you *have* died, haven't you? He's afraid because he's got so much to lose—you, and Paul—even his own double. He's full of fears like that. His universe is you and Paul, quite simply; and that ship he's lost. Himself, of course; but he's sure I'd retaliate on you. He can't conceive of the universe without him in it; can't conceive of your survival if he didn't exist. Responsibility for the whole universe. That kind of thinking's very remote in you. . . . Not that you don't care," it said, settling crosslegged to the floor. "Just that you don't think in terms of being anything but alone. Not universal like Rafe; just solitary. The men take care of you; they look for nothing from you, so you think. You'd defend them if you got the chance. But you expect no chances, for you, or them. On the other hand—you've died once, you think; and that didn't impress you much. It didn't affect you. You've still got yourself; and that's your universe."

"Sure," she said. An icy worm crawled somewhere at her gut. "You got anything to do besides this? Let's see your face, why not?"

"You don't like me using this shape. Your brother's—your husband's; that you can tolerate. *This* bothers you."

"I hate your guts. Surprising?"

"And now you're scared. Something's got inside."

She was. She stared at the thing eye to eye and it had her own most determined look.

"Go to hell," she said.

"Your strategy is self-defense. Around that you arrange your priorities. I understand this."

It had made her angry. It had made her afraid. It had indeed gotten through. *Stupid,* she thought, *stupid to debate this thing.* That it had *her,* that it lived inside her head, made her afraid not to listen to it, and that was a trap. She shut that worry down, assumed its own crosslegged pose in mockery. "Suppose we see your face. The way you really are."

"Clever," it said.

"I shut you off, didn't I?"

It smiled, her own most wicked smile. "Shut me down cold," it said.

"That brain reacts—mirror image to mine."

"When it's on the same track. *Think of children.*"

Back in her lap. She went off her balance, confused.

"You don't like the idea," it said. "Rafe's upset you didn't live to have the kids he wanted so, he's upset and ashamed he's upset, and won't mention it to you because he thinks in the first place you're grieved at losing that chance and secondly that you'd think it affects his care for you. I know. I felt it quite distinctly."

"Thank him for me," she said hoarsely. "Spare him my opinions."

"You did. Spare him that, I mean. Your sex bears the young, with some pain; more than that—the time. You bear one at a time; there had to be several. It meant going to *Ajax,* being absent from everything you valued, for a long period of your lifespan; it meant inactivity; it meant kids' noise and helplessness, which you don't like; it meant pretending for years and years that you were happy when you weren't, because your misery would affect the men, and cause them pain, and affect the kids, and ruin all the rest of the years you had left to live. Everything Rafe's worked for—depends on you. And you hate it."

"Don't tell them that."

"This is the center where no one comes. Death can't affect it. This is the strategy: silence, and to strike from this place where nothing can come. This virtue. This anger that sustains you. You know your limits. You cherish no illusions. But I'm here."

"Welcome in," she said, staring through it. "Now there are two of us. You want a fight? I'll give you one."

"Yes," it said. "I know. But I would win. I have, before. I destroyed that version of you. It was no longer whole."

"Fine," she said. There was a knot in her throat that made talking painful. "That was kind of you."

"Humor," it said.

"Absolutely."

"I want your help," it said.

She looked at it, a sudden shortening of focus, a centering of hate. *"Do* you?"

"You don't fully understand," it said, "what these versions are. They're alive."

"That one was?" She moved her eyes where Paul had lain, unconscious on the floor. "You *killed* it? *You want my help?*"

"He. That version died in his sleep, without pain. He can die—infinitely often. No," the doppelganger said, lifting her hand. "That wasn't a threat. I'm explaining what you are. You have a certain integrity, right now. You're unique, much more flexible than the template I have in storage. You've learned. That version of Paul I twice destroyed —never waked after the wreck. The one I sent you to keep you content, that one was from the same template; and it came to consciousness with you all settled in your state. You brought it—gently up to date; it's more stable as a consequence. Paul, you know, doesn't like shocks. He relies on you in these circumstances. He needs your flexibility. Your expertise as spacers, greater than his own. Oh, I know—you're lost. That's why the first Paul ran off. He leaned on you and you didn't provide the prop. So he leaned on himself. And he ran."

"O my God."

"No, indeed you didn't get the same Paul back. And you did, in one important sense. The one you have now is healthier. He still belongs to you. The other one, the one that ran, has diverged—considerably. You thanked me for destroying your damaged selves. But Paul's first copy was damaged too. It's not a Paul you'd understand. And a stray version of Rafe exists, that's gone way off. Rafe has his weaknesses. That's why I'm talking to you. The stable one. The one with the solid core. The only one it hasn't got. Yet."

"It. What—*it?*"

"This ship has a lot of passengers. One of them."

"And who are you?"

"Kepta. Kepta's what to call me."

"You're in charge?"

"Captain would be close. I'm going to copy you again. It's the best defense. That there'll be one version of you neither naïve nor—if things go wrong—corrupt. It will hurt, Jillan. It's not my choice. It's just your nature."

It was gone.

And the pain began.

"</> knows," said = < + > = = < − > = =. "</> knows < >'re disarranged."

< > was not surprised at the Cannibal's report. < > stayed quiet now, digesting what < > had learned, while in the lab, with another part of < >'s mind, < > was quite busy.

"Move us," said <ʌ>, anxiously, from elsewhere in the ship. <ʌ> feared the Cannibal and stayed far away. "Move us from this place. Others of this species may come."

"No," < > said, "not yet."

<ʌ> raged and wept, fearful for <ʌ>self. <ʌ> was very old, and very fond of <ʌ>self, besides being slightly mad, and <ʌ> skulked off, with ‖000‖ slinking after in growing despair.

"</> knows what < > have done," <ʌ> said again, turning back.

"</> knows," said another, unexpected voice. It was </>self. </> had ventured to the limits of </>'s security, that line across which < > did not go. This intrusion into < >'s affairs was purest insolence, demonstrating </>'s strength; but demonstrating impotence as well: </> had met a limit </> could not pass.

But </> brought a companion who had no such disabilities. < > saw this. "Paul," < > addressed Paul One, which hung back, twined with crippled Rafe-mind, the one that </> had worn. Paul had acquired new pieces, shadow-limbs, extensions in the dark, at least three arms, maybe four; and legs as well.

The Paul-mind said something, garbled like itself. ". . . . fear," came out. "jillan rafe bastard want come now . . ."

"Not very articulate," < > said. The template < > was making was complete. With deliberation < > released the subject, dismissed her out of reach and fronted </>'s vexation with insouciance.

Gentle, human arms were about her, light shone above her, and for a moment Jillan believed in both implicitly, having no wish to move at all, only to be, and not to think.

"Jillan," Paul's voice called. His fingers touched her face, brushed back a stubborn lock of hair—he often did that small thing, of mornings, to wake her up. Tears leaked between her lashes; but the pain was gone, just gone, as if it had never been, hard even to remember now. She opened her eyes and blinked at Paul's face, at two of Rafe's, one of the twins like Paul, dimmed by the lights; the other, Rafe's living self.

Her men, she thought, exhausted. All three of them safe, here among *Lindy*'s pathetic pieces. She sat up and held to Paul's shoulder, hung on it like a drifter to a hold in null, and gazed at both her brothers, the living and the one neither live nor dead.

"You all right?" Rafe asked, a rusty, painful sound.

"What happened to your voice?"

"Had a bad while," he said. "Over now. I'm not hurt. You?"

She nodded. Her mind felt adrift in fragments. There was too much, too much they did not know. She tightened her grip on Paul's bare shoulder and drew a deep and shaky breath. "I'm all right," she said. "You know somebody named Kepta?"

"Yes," said her living brother in that strained, hoarse voice. "I know him."

"Him." The mental shift made her think again. "Her. It. Whatever. Whatever it really is." She slid her hand down to Paul's and clenched its solidity. "I'm all right. You?"

"Fine," Paul said. "Fine," said Rafe, her Rafe, the one the light shone through. She felt a chill—*how be sure it's them, mine, not something else?*—as if the floor were falling away, the gossamer-carpet floor her body could not feel. She stared at them and froze a moment, then drew her limbs under her and sat apart, pulling her hand from Paul's, resting her forehead on her knee.

"Destroy all of them," [] said, one of ten of []kind, one of a chorus of voices, hundreds of outraged protests which < > ignored, occupied as < > was. Paul-mind had retreated, with < / >, to that place where < / > was firmly in charge.

It was too late to recover Paul One, < > knew. Paul One was quite, quite beyond any reason. More, he had gained a certain wariness, which indicated that his immunity against shutdown was increasing.

< > could not keep < / > from the controls long. There would be distractions. < > knew.

"*Aaaaiiiiiii!*" ((())) wailed, irreverent of boundaries, passed < > and hid, pathetic in ((()))'s disturbance. But ((())) had never been particularly self-restrained before ((())) slipped from sanity. "Aiii," ((())) mourned, in short, painful sobs, "aiii, aiii."

"Accurate," said < >.

"Jillan," Rafe said, unable to touch her—he reached, that was all that he could do; and every movement hurt his sprains. "You're sure that you're all right?"

"Sure," she said in a hoarse small voice. "Rafe—how do you know it's me?"

A chill went over him. "Your asking makes it likely," he said after a moment. "Doesn't it? It's you. Question is—how far down the line?"

"You know, then."

"I know," he said.

She ran a hand through her hair, disturbing its disorder, blinked at him, at the ones insubstantial like herself. "Paul? Rafe?"

"What?" Rafe Two answered.

"You know—both of you—about the copies that exist—"

"I saw my double," Paul said. "Didn't all of us?"

"That question's always worth asking," she said to Paul. *"Didn't all of us?"* Her eyes came back to Rafe, haunted. "You know what dawns on me? That even I don't know which I am. It copied me. Which one left? Which stayed? It's all academic, isn't it? That copy's back there, and if it's awake, it's scared as I'd be. Doing everything I'd do, thinking every thought, because it is—me. I am there. And here. That's the way it works."

"For God's sake, Jillan—"

"Rafe, I talked—*talked*—I'm not even sure of that . . . to something that calls itself Kepta; it's in charge. There's more than one."

"You're sure of that."

"It said there were a lot of passengers. A lot. And, Paul—Paul, that copy of you we saw—one of them's got it. Got one of you, Rafe. This Kepta says they've gotten—damaged somehow. That they're maybe—dangerous."

"Jillan," Rafe Two said, sharp and brittle. "Jillan, save it. Our brother's not involved in this. He's leaving."

"Leaving?"

"Tell it to me," Rafe said to her, hearing things that made far too much sense. Jillan looked afraid, glancing from one to the other of them. Paul's face was stark with panic. "How—dangerous?"

"What's this about leaving?" Jillan asked him; and when he said nothing, looked at Rafe Two.

"It's given him a chance," Rafe Two said. "It'll take him to Paradise, a capsule of some kind, a signal—it'll drop him off."

"You believe that?" Jillan asked, looking round at him.

"What did Kepta say to you?" Rafe persisted in his turn.

"It's the best promise we've got," the doppelganger said in his, crouching there, hands loose between his knees. "It says it's moving on, going elsewhere. No more concern with the whole human race. Wants to drop off our living component, it does. Maybe before his food runs out. I don't know why. I don't care. I've told Rafe I'd just as soon he was out of here."

"Rafe," Rafe said, "mind your business. Jillan, what's going on?"

"Nothing," she said, tight and quick.

"Don't give me nothing. It's got—what, the first of Paul? The one that ran. And me. Which me?"

"I don't know." She shook her head, with panic in her eyes. "I've no idea."

"Early or late copy?"

"I don't know. It didn't tell me that."

"It's not your business," Rafe Two said. "You're leaving. You're getting off this ship."

"It's got to get there first." Rafe felt his heart beating double time, looked from one to the other of them, Jillan, Rafe—Paul, whose panic was all but tangible.

"You take any ticket out of here you've got," Jillan said. "Look—Rafe: you're only one of you. You understand? I'm not alone. Paul's not. You're still with us. You'll be with us—in duplicate."

"She's right," his doppelganger said, putting out his hand as if to touch his arm. "You're superfluous—aren't you? You take any way you can off this ship. We've already settled that."

Rafe sat still, staring at all of them, wiped his hand across his lip.

"He's right," Paul said from over by the wall, in a small and steady voice. "You're the one that's really at risk. Get out if you've got a choice. We want you to do that. We want to know you're safe."

The voice lingered. Paul's body was gone. All of them were, suddenly, as if they had never been. There was only the corridor, the remnants, the pieces of *Lindy*.

"That's not enough!" Rafe shouted, in his ruined whisper of a voice. He looked up at the warted, serpentine ceiling, the trail of lights and raised his fists at it. *"Kepta—"* His voice gave way, beyond audibility. "Kepta," he tried again. "Kepta, send them back!"

There was a passing wail, loud, devastatingly loud. He clapped his hands over his ears until the worst of it had gone.

Then was silence, long silence. He sat down, aching, in the vacant chair at *Lindy*'s console. He passed his hands over controls, the few that worked, and looked at the starfield vid gave him.

He knew where he was now. He had confirmed Altair, and Vega burning bright, the two great beacons of the dark near human space, virtually touching from this perspective. The myriad, myriad others, the few wan human stars. Sol . . . was out of field.

That way? he wondered. *Is that the direction it means to go? Is that what it's telling me?* He could see Paradise, a dim, common star, nothing much, the kind mankind preferred.

He switched on the com. "Kepta," he said, patiently, watching lights flicker, reckoning it might be heard. "Kepta, you want to talk to me?"

No answer.

He bowed his head on the console, looked up finally at the vid. Nothing changed. Inertial at 1/10 C. Drifting, after jump, in some place off human routes.

No one would find them. God help whoever did. God help the whole species if someone did.

He wiped at his eyes, his cheek resting against the metal console. To leave this place—to let it take Paul and Jillan on—

To let it have himself, in infinite series, erasing what it liked, keeping what it wanted until he was whatever Kepta chose—

"Kepta, talk to me."

And after a long while of silence: "Kepta, you want to discuss this?"

"I don't think," someone said behind him, "you'd recognize my voice on that radio."

He spun the chair about, wincing with sore ribs and joints, blinked at the dimming of the lights, at Jillan standing there.

"Don't do that." His hoarseness betrayed him, cracked in his disturbance.

"Come up behind you?" Kepta asked in Jillan's fair clear tones.

"Her."

"Use this shape, you mean? It was convenient. Most recent, even more than yours. I don't like to partition off more than I have to, or struggle with a mind too long out of date."

"You going—where? Vega, maybe? Somewhere near?"

"Might," Kepta said. "Might not."

"You won't say."

"I don't know," Kepta said. "I haven't decided that. Is that why you called me?"

"Jillan said—there was trouble on the ship."

"There may be."

"Look, are we going to Paradise?"

"I told you that we were."

"*What* trouble?"

"I don't see it concerns you."

"Dammit—I want to know."

Jillan's eyes looked up at him, with Jillan's innocence, beneath a fringe of disordered hair. "What difference can it make?"

"I'm not going. I'm not leaving this. I want to know."

"Not leaving the ship?"

"No more than you ever meant me to." His voice broke down. "You set this up. Didn't you?"

"No. But between this mind and your own—I figured that you'd stay."

He gazed at his sister's shape, untouchable, something it hurt even to curse. "You always right?"

"No. That would be unbearable. Besides—we need only delay your trip. We can settle this thing, if you'll cooperate. Then I'll take you to Paradise. Or anywhere you like. We'll make it reciprocal. I get your wholehearted assistance. You name your destination. I'll take you there. Reward. We do share that concept."

"Paradise is good enough." His voice broke down, came out small and diminished, and he hated it. *Jillan,* his eyes kept telling him. The mind inside was half hers at least, knowing him with her thoroughness, memories shared from infancy, childhood, all their lives. "What do you want—another copy? That help?"

"It might. But taking it so soon might weaken you considerably. It might even kill you. And I won't."

"I don't mistake that for sentiment."

The Jillan-figure paused, its hazel transparent eyes quite earnest. "No," it said. "Disadvantage outweighs advantage. Trans-species, transactions can be explained like that, in motiveless simplicity. Advantage and disadvantage. Facts and acts. True reasons, trans-species, rarely make full sense. Even basic ones. Suffice it to say I can use this simulacrum; I just partition. It takes very little attention. On the other hand, if you tried my mind—it would be the other problem. You'd probably not wake up: large box, small content."

"Real modest."

"Factual. I'm complex." Kepta diminished in brightness. "You have your qualities. I don't say they're unique. The combination of them is. In all the universe, the snowflakes, grains of sand, chemical combinations, the DNA that makes up, for instance, Rafael Lewis Murray—" The voice faded too. "—not to mention his experience at any given moment—the chance of finding anything exactly duplicated is most remote. Haven't you seen that on this ship? Infinity is always in you, Rafael Murray, and the other way around. . . ."

It was gone, faded into silence.

It was Jillan he found in the dark, or who found him, starlike striding across the nowhere plain.

"Rafe," she said when she reached him, in that gentle tone that was very much her own.

But Rafe Two was wary, having landed without preface in this nowhere place, alone and unprepared.

"Jillan?" he asked of Jillan-shape, and knew, by the splitsecond it had hesitated to answer him, that it was not. "You want—what?" he asked. "What do you want from me?"

"You know that," Kepta said. "You know a lot of things by now. Your state's become valuable to me again."

Rafe-Mind, Paul One, all woven together, like the multiplicity of limbs: it moved in shambling misery back to the territory </> owned.

"I," it mourned, "I, I, I—" not knowing what that *I* meant until </> took the Rafe-mind up and relieved Paul of carrying it.

</> shuddered despite </>self as </> extended a portion of </>'s mind and straightened things. </> forced Rafe-mind to resume the configurations </> remembered, and went on rearranging.

Rafe screamed, and took in </>'s partitioned intrusion—grew quiet then, carrying on his reflexive functions, beginning to re-sort and gather on his own.

</> left him then, and Rafe at least went on functioning. Rafe-mind had new configurations, certain amputations, a certain dependency. "He's yours," </> said to Paul.

Paul felt of it and insinuated a portion of himself, imitating </> in this.

"Be careful," </> said, though pleased. "It will deform. Go in more gently this time."

Paul derived memories, sorted them and reconfigured himself. He had learned. </> taught him—many things. Self-defense was one. To enter another simulacrum was another.

He handled Rafe-mind this time with some skill: </>'s rearrangements had slipped him past Rafe-mind's defenses in some regards, given him a new chance at others.

He looked about him with increasing confidence. He knew = = = = in = = = ='s various segments and knew that all such were dangerous, but he was stronger. He knew ((())), that ((())) was mad, and was unafraid of the sometime howling that streaked panic-stricken through the passages. He knew [] and <v>, <⌃> and |:|, which began—justifiably—to be afraid of him.

Paul, he still thought of himself. Paul One was something which adequately described him, since he was the inheritor, oldest and wisest of all Pauls. About destroying his other simulacrum he had no compunction whatsoever, no more than he had had in his former state for shed hair or the trimmings of his fingernails.

He sought both Rafes and Jillan with a different intent—remembering how they had sought him out back on Fargone station, wanting his money, his brains, his back, and most of all his genes for the getting of other Murrays. He had let himself be used in every way there was, and that thought burned in him like acid.

He could still forgive. He could forgive it all, on his own terms, in their perpetual atonement. He would no longer take their orders, no more orders from Jillan and from Rafe, no more belonging to them; but them to him, belonging the way this Rafe-mind did. It was afraid of him.

He stroked it, taking pleasure in its fear and dependency, as if it were the original.

His own template he meant to destroy, along with his duplicate. He would be unique. There would be no more duplicates to rival him. He had become a predator, and wanted, for practical reasons, nothing in the universe exactly like himself.

He developed wishes very much like $</>$ and was well satisfied with that outlook. He knew most that happened elsewhere on the ship. $</>$ spoke to him and kept him well informed.

He knew, for instance, that the living Rafe had just made a mistake, in that territory too well defended for $</>$ to breach as yet. He had let $<>$ get a very dangerous template, one that trusted everything far too much. Paul ached to have that Rafe, in particular.

"Patience," $</>$ said. "Not yet. $</>$ promise you."

$<>$, across the ship, was shifting to another simulacrum, and Paul knew that too.

"Attack," Paul wished $</>$, constant on this theme, and [] was interested.

"Not yet," $</>$ insisted.

"$<>$'s chosen you to use," [] said, prodding at him.

"And $<>$'s having trouble configuring it," $</>$ reported, to Paul's keen satisfaction.

"It would fight," Paul said; and in an access of passion: "Take $<>$ now. Now's a chance for us."

"Be patient," $</>$ insisted still. "$<>$ will get $<>$self into difficulty sooner or later. That's inevitable. Then all the rest will come to us. Won't they, Rafe?"

The simulacrum shivered, best substitute they had. "I'll come," it said, having difficulty distinguishing I from they, "I have to."

Paul was satisfied. Rafe's fear was sensual to him; gender had

stopped mattering, along with other things, but sex was more important than it had ever been.

In that regard he shared one tendency with $====$. He aspired
to multiplicity. He was not large, not like $</>$. He knew his level
and his limits, and had no designs on $<>$. Being born a stationer he
had never thought about command. He aimed at simple competence,
to function well within the whole—and he had his place all picked out,
in something very large indeed, which understood all his appetites.

"I want to talk with you," Paul's voice said; and Paul blinked,
suddenly without his companions, alone, in the dark, with his version
of himself.

"Who are you?" he asked. He felt his nonexistent heart, another
insanity—dead, his heart kept beating. It sped with fear; his skin felt
the flush of adrenalin, and he faced this thing in a panic close to shock.
"Which are you?"

"Kepta," his doppelganger said. "The others know me. You're quite
safe. You want to sit down, Paul?"

He sat down where he was, in the vast and shapeless dark. He set
his hands on his crossed ankles and stared at his mirrored shape which
took up a pose very like his own.

"You're the hardest," the doppelganger said, "the most difficult to
occupy. I ruined several of you with Rafe's memories; one with Jillan's. Two went to pieces of their own accord. Keep yourself calm. I
assure you I won't hurt you."

"You will," Paul said, remembering what the others had been
through. "Let's get that on the table, why don't we? You want me the
way I am. You want a copy of me, a sane one; and it's going to hurt
like hell. Can't we get on with that?"

"You've stabilized," it said, "considerably. You're quite complex of
your type. Your mind goes off at tangents, travels quite rapidly com-
pared to the others. You make fantasies of elaborate and deliberate
sort. Not the most elaborate. There's an entity aboard—I could never
say the name in frequencies you'd hear—who sits and modifies, nothing else. I'm not quite sure it's sane, but it's bothered no one yet."

"Cut it," Paul said. "Why should I talk to you at all?"

"I want to find out what I can. To learn anything that may have bearing on what you are. There's trouble, understand, and one of your versions is in the middle of it."

"Good."

"No. Not good at all. Not for your sake. Least of all for Jillan and Rafe."

"How?"

"Their freedom. Their existence, for that matter. That's at risk. Not to mention your own.—Stay calm. Keep calm."

His breath was short. He locked his arms about his knees, conscious of nakedness, of vulnerability, of rank, raw panic with this thing. "Nothing of me would ever hurt them."

"Yes. It would. You have more to your mind; you have—you'd call it—a darker side."

"Not against them."

"Especially against them."

"You read minds, do you?"

"Only this one. The one I'm in. It reacts to things I think. It's painful. Quite painful. I can feel this body's processes going wild. Give me help, Paul. It's going out on me."

He blinked, saw the rigid muscles, the evidence of stress in corded arms, saw it shiver—felt ashamed of its mirrored weakness.

It faded out, in black.

Dead? he wondered. He wiped at nonexistent sweat, at a blurring in his eyes. His heart was still going fit to burst.

Fear killed it. Mine.

It came back again, materialized sitting cross-legged in front of him.

"I had to make a new one," Kepta said. "You see what I mean."

"It just broke apart."

"It wasn't a small stress I put on it. Can we keep off that subject? I'd rather think of where you came from for the moment. Fargone. Please—don't panic.—Paul, do something."

"What?"

"Anything."

"Like get the hell out of here?"

"Keep talking."

"Where's the rest of us? What *is* this place?"

"A ship." The mirror-image looked more relaxed. "That's where you are, you understand. I think Rafe and Jillan have told you some things. I want you to keep one fact very much in mind, keep thinking on it constantly, even at the worst."

"What's that?"

"Love. They love you, Paul, no matter how dangerous you are. Never lose that thought."

"Huh," he said, shook his head in embarrassment. "Murderer gone maudlin. You killed me, damn you; killed Jillan—"

"It's true; don't doubt that they love you, don't doubt it for a moment. It's very important. It's the most important thing, isn't it? It's your whole universe."

He felt heat in his face, utter shame.

"I know," it said with his mouth, looking steadily out of his eyes at him, with his squarish, stubborn face. "I'm absolutely sure what you're doing here. Love describes it, why you came, why you worked all those years with them at things that frighten you. To avoid Fargone mines. That was one reason: being afraid of the deep and dark, where your mother died—shot in riot. Riot. That leads places—"

"Shut up."

"But most of all—you want company. You want to give and get love. You think there's something inherently wrong in that. It's not a rational transaction. And you value rationality; your species does, yes, I know—while you, you operate from the gut; that's the word, isn't it? From the gut. You find this embarrassing?"

"Maybe," he said, because it was, because saying anything else was too complicated and even worse. He looked off into the dark to evade its eyes and had to look back again.

"You rate Rafe and Jillan," it said, "higher than yourself. *Braver*, you would say, because their actions come more often from rationality. Rafe-mind thinks that's nonsense, but never mind—you rate them smarter, too. That's difficult for me to judge, even having used all three of you. You've taken Rafe for your senior, though the age difference is small. It's not the real reason you have him for superior, though it's the one you prefer to use. You acknowledge the same superiority in Jillan, who's your age, and you've partitioned off a small resentment for this, much stronger toward Jillan, who evokes strongest feelings in you. Your gender is physically the stronger. Your emotional faculty equates strength of all kinds with fitness to mate. But many individuals are stronger and better of your species; you really rely on opportunity—a contradiction at the root of many insecurities."

"Every man has that."

"To Rafe—it's *ship*. In him, your kind of thinking is very short range: he'd only think that way on the docks. In specific. Not constantly measuring himself. He knows what would make him fit to mate with fit mates—A ship. He's lost that now, and that hurt him; but he's too busy yet to think of that. He has other priorities. He *knows* his measure. He's got the universe to save . . . in his own self. And that comes first. While Jillan—"

"Leave her out of this."

"Why? Why leave her out? That's an important question. Isn't it?"

"Just don't."

"Don't consider her? She'd resent that, you know. Do you understand, she thinks like Rafe—about the ship. With it, she was merchanter. Free to take whatever mates she fancied. The one freedom she would have—outside the children. Outside childbearing. She was happy in that prospect. She looked forward to it. But *ship* drives her, the way it drives Rafe. She went to you—your money, your attachment—your friendship—"

"Stop it, dammit."

"—for Rafe's sake. For hers. *Responsibility*. It drives her in a different way, to do unpleasant things. She feels quite powerless in the most important regards. This marriage—this permanency—took away the one reward she had reserved for herself. That too she did. For the ship."

"O God."

"You resent her every competency. And Rafe's."

"No."

"At heart, you suspect your validity. You resented the thought of the Murray name on all your offspring; you gave in on that. You gave up your money to them. You rely on them for smallest decisions; and you need them—emotionally. You have no remote goals like theirs. Yours is very simple: to validate yourself—continually. And to do this, you attached to those who had no weakness in your eyes. You wanted a larger thing to belong to. In them, you found it. You have to understand that about yourself. You do have to belong."

"I know," he said. There was nothing else to say to that, nothing at all.

"You've always doubted your importance. Your grandmother was born in a lab and had a number tattooed on her hand. You rarely saw your mother. She supported you by mine work. You're not sure whether that was love or duty. She never said. She died and left you a station share, which gave you the ability to live in some comfort. But your species needs attachments of stronger sort. Rafe was one. And Jillan. They were your shelter in youth. They ran wild on the docks. You envied them—not their freedom, but their unity. And they made you a part of them. Adult needs grew into that. For you—there were no other possibilities."

"Why don't we try for that copy you need?"

"No. Go on thinking on that point. It's a crucial one for you. There's ambiguity there. You went into a very dangerous situation; mining, which you hate; in a very unsafe ship; left all your comforts; exchanged all values you had for this one return, that you give and get love from both of them. That seems an important point. Doesn't it?"

He drew a deep breath, feeling naked in more ways than physically. "Yes," he said.

"Vulnerability is upsetting to you."

"To anyone."

"Upset is itself a vulnerability."

"Is there some point to this?"

"Oh, yes. There is. I fell victim to that aspect of you myself. Your simulacra were all painful to me. And I avoided that upset. I drew an unwarranted conclusion, that you would not adapt. Rafe did warn me. Your survival should have warned me. Your runaway copy evaded every danger but one. That's quite a defense you have."

"Sure."

"There is aggression in you. There is—what you would call that dark side; secrets you keep partitioned. So you understand a little of what I do when I occupy a mind. I partition off those parts of me that would be incompatible. But you don't have as fine a control on that partitioning; Jillan *uses* hers; Rafe operates in simplicity: his secrets are all little ones, excepting one. Excepting one. But you—You deliberately disorganize yourself, destroying connections—like now, like this mind's trying to do, and I won't press it. Remember that one thing. Remember what I told you was important to remember. That's how the first Paul Gaines went wrong."

"What—went wrong?"

"Mad. From your viewpoint, he's quite mad. Pull out everything you hold behind those barriers and you'll know in what respect. I know you, Paul. There's no aspect of this mind I haven't been through, nothing I haven't handled. I've killed several of you doing it, at some cost to me."

"What do you want from me?"

"I want you to deal with Paul One. It's very likely that you're the only one that can both reach and affect him."

"You can't?" Wit started working again, and seized on that hint of limitation. *Learn something—bring it back to them—*

—prove myself—The truth of it jarred.

"I'll be—otherwise occupied. I know that I will be. And if you break down, Paul—if you do break down, it's very likely I'll have to wipe the templates out. That's death. For Rafe, and you, and Jillan. Real death, not a power-down. There are several worse things that could happen. Remote, but possible."

"What's that?"

"One, that you'd become his. The other Paul's. That he'd have all of you, and the templates, to do with as he pleases. That could happen— if I should go under. And it's possible I could. It's always possible. Believe me, destroying the templates against that event—would be charity."

He clenched hands that felt cold in the absence of all cold, swallowed against a knot that was not there. "And if you're lying, all the way—what then, Kepta?"

"You might take the chance and assume that I'm lying. But you've seen that first version of yourself. Did you like it? Did it look healthy?"

"No," he said. "No."

"Do you want to fight this thing? Or had you rather go now? Which will you choose? To get back, to go to sleep? I can arrange that. Or I can tell you what you have to do, to avoid catastrophe."

"What's that?" he asked. It did not seem himself asking, as if he watched from some great distance where he had gone for safety. "What am I supposed to do?"

"Understand it. Understand what that first version, what every version of you has behind every partition of its mind. Understand *yourself.* If there's one weakness it will find it; if there's one doubt, it's going to discover it. Think of those partitioned things. Think through all your mind until it has no seams, no joining-places, no contradictions at all. Did you know you enjoy giving pain? That you fear the dark? Do you know that Rafe uses you, even while he loves you? That you want Jillan to be less than she is? That you want to be feared?"

"That's a lie."

"Not a lie. It's the obverse, the wellspring of all the strengths you have. You come from a place, from Fargone; I remember. Hundreds of thousands of your kind are crowded together there. You exist in stress and refrain from every hostile thought and violence. You partition off these things. You live by active denial of them. That other Paul, that you ran—has no partitions. The moment you meet him—neither will you."

He stared into eyes the like of his, feeling ice lodged in his gut.

"Let's talk about sex, Paul."

"What about it?"

"Defensive," Kepta said. "You wish most of all you had clothes. That really bothers you."

"I haven't got the urge. Haven't. Won't." He felt a sweat break out that could not possibly exist. "I don't think I'm likely to."

"Rafe feels these reactions, but generalized and rarely in this place. Worry—fear—kinship—these suppress the drive."

"So does dying."

"Does it?" Kepta asked.

He stared at Kepta, recalling what it knew, what it remembered.

"The clothes," Kepta said, "the clothes. An inconvenience in the templates, but a very important protection to you. Jillan's bothered least. Rafe—inconvenienced. You're terrified. Aren't you, Paul?"

He said nothing, only looked it in the eyes.

"Physiology betrays you," Kepta said. "This body can react—in many ways. It will. You fear it will . . . and Rafe—has stopped being . . . *brother* . . ."

"Damn you."

". . . become—*rival,* in this dark aspect. In several senses. So has she."

"They're better," he said at last, between the two of them. "They're better than I am. Aren't they?"

"I can't judge."

"Can't you?"

"I won't be there. You will. In this—it's not better, Paul. It's what survives."

"It can't all rest on me. Dammit, give me—give me more than that. . . ."

Kepta rose, straightened, unfolding in midair so that he stood. He held out his hand. "I can't. Take my hand. I'll send you back to familiar referents . . . after I've made a copy. This is a valuable point with you, this moment. If you disintegrate hereafter, I might try—perhaps once more with you. Only perhaps. I won't risk the ship. You mustn't depend on anything but yourself. Remember what I told you is important."

He thought back, and another thought came, far colder. "You know my mind inside and out. More than lying—isn't it possible you know how to manipulate us? You know just what strings to pull, and when. You're not learning things from this. You're *moving* us—to do the things you want."

Kepta's brows lifted slowly; as slowly, the mouth assumed a grudging smile. "Of all of you—you're the first to challenge me on that. Of course I am. I see why the others value you, Paul Gaines. You do have surprises. And now you have a choice. Your hand . . . if you will."

He held it out, repulsed as Kepta's closed on his in a dry, temperatureless grip. Kepta's clasp was strong, like living metal, perilous in its potentiality.

"Don't close down," he said. "Let *go!*"—as the air around them dissolved and whirled in a blur of his own glowing limbs. *"No!"* he cried.

It let go.

Pain shot through him then.

It was worse than he had expected, and longer.

Far longer.

"Kepta!" he cried, over and over again, "Jillan, Rafe! O God, God, God—!"

—thinking he was dying. He remembered death.

But he awoke in tranquility, in Rafe's nest of *Lindy*'s parts.

"You all right?" Rafe Two was leaning over him. Jillan wiped his brow and for a moment he lay there.

He stopped breathing for a moment, experimentally; started it up again, not for air: for the comfort of it.

"Paul, are you all right?"

He let Rafe help him sit, hugged Jillan to him, her head against his shoulder. There was light. Light all about him. He cherished it, looking about him. He saw Rafe One standing there, helpless-looking in his solidity.

"It got its copy," he said to them all. "That was what it wanted. A lot better than the last, I think."

No, he had screamed. He remembered that suddenly.

Remembered other things.

He had taken terror into the experience. That, along with his self-knowledge and self-disgust.

That was his backup. Flawed.

Chapter Eight

There was silence in the corridor, among *Lindy*'s pieces, the silence of waiting, when everything had been said, when the only needs were his own, and Rafe moved about those when he must, under the eyes of those whose remaining necessity was breathing, and that only because they could not forget to do it.

To eat, to drink—these things seemed cruel to do while they witnessed; to sleep—Rafe did sleep as he sat against the wall, a nodding of his head, a panicked look to see whether they were still there.

"All accounted for," said Rafe Two, who read all his body language with more skill than Jillan ever could. "None of us have been anywhere."—Meaning they were all intact, and as much themselves as they had been when he went to sleep.

"I'd think," said Jillan, "it could have gotten its business together by now."

"It's waiting for something else," Rafe said.

"What would it be waiting for?" asked Paul.

Rafe shrugged.

"You know something we don't?" asked Rafe Two.

He shrugged again, wiped his face, got up and went about his toilet —shaved, because he needed it.

"Not sorry to miss that." Rafe Two perched on the counter edge, transparent and only partly phasing with it. In the mirror, Jillan and Paul leaned against the console of *Lindy*'s dead panel, watching him with proprietary interest.

"I wish you wouldn't stare," he said.

"Sorry," Jillan said. "It's the only action going."

Rafe-nothing crept along in the dark, blind as he had become. At times he thought he wept; but maybe that was illusion like the dark, for his hands felt nothing when he touched his face.

He had seen horror. Some of it still lived inside, and consciousness came and went; but he had seen his chance and slipped away, crawling in the dark.

He had had many limbs. And few. Now he had no understanding what shape was his. He only traveled as he could, as far as he could, and he supposed that limbs took him there.

Then something began to move beside him in the void, shadowy at first, with the outlines of some leggy, rippling beast. It brushed against him and the touch of it sent a shock through all his nerves.

He screamed. *"Aii! Aiii!"* it shrieked back at him, which so unnerved him he rolled aside from it and sat staring at this nest of coils and legs that swayed closer and closer, towering above him in black-glistening segments outlined in yellow light.

"Help," it cried, "help, help—" It was not himself which understood this, but one of those ruptured areas of his mind, one of those places that hung in painful ruin, like threads that went into the dark, into inside-out perspectives.

He stared at it, and it oozed from its heap and surrounded him with its coils. He heard it sobbing, felt the shock of its nibbling up these stray threads, and the tears ran on his face.

"Come, come, come," it wished him. He understood it through these threads. He recalled in horror what he was, and what pursued. "Get up and run," the worm-thing wailed. "It will take you. Run!"

He wished to run. He tried to. A murkish glow came about them and the worm-thing fled.

"No," said Paul's chill voice above him, and a firm grasp gathered him up again.

He wept, having again more than several limbs, being in pain, while that monstrous shape enfolded all of them, in a welter of disturbed perspective. It swallowed up the threads, and he was blind.

"Paul," he tried to say, "Paul, that isn't right."

"Rafael Murray," the tall man said, taking him by the hand, bend-ing down to their level. "Jillan—"—taking hers, so they knew some-thing bad would come: nothing good ever came of Welfare strangers, not especially official ones in expensive suits, and he wished this man away with the horror of foreknowledge. "There's been an accident," the man would say next. "Out in the belt—"

That was what Paul did to him for revenge. It used his memories, put him back in that time until he had no more recollection of any worm-thing.

"No," the shining girl said, the star-jumper who had come to Fargone docks in her wealth and security. "No." And he could see in her eyes the longhauler's prejudice against insystemers, that he would ever approach the likes of her and offer to sleepover with her, in this place longhaulers frequented and insystemers dared not come. She looked him up and down. She was all of, maybe, seventeen at most, unsure and offended in her inexperience. "Better get out of here," she said.

And he: "My name's Murray."

"There a ship that name?"

"There was," he said, realizing it had been so small, so long ago, even spacers had forgotten. "Lindy was her name."

Dead ship. He saw the pity. "Buy me a drink," she said with forti-tude. And maybe because she knew he had so little: "No, you have one on me."

"No thanks," he said. Desire had cooled in him. It was the first approach he had ever made to a woman of spacer-kind, after weeks of nerving himself. He guessed he might be her first, and even pitied her courage. She wanted her first with someone better. Someone memora-ble. She was good-hearted and would take him and never talk about it. Ever. The wound in both of them would live for years . . . whatever he did now. "No. Give it to someone else," he said. And he walked away.

</> was, at depth, dismayed at the near escape of Rafe-mind, <> detected it clear across the ship.

"Good for you," <> sent the damaged Rafe-mind in a pulse transcending boundaries. *"Good for you, "*—in terms Rafe-mind might understand.

And a part of <>self, that portion which had several times participated in Rafe-mind—stirred.

"Good for me," it said.

And foreseeing crisis, <> raised a simulacrum, and pushed it to the light.

The pain stopped. Rafe caught his breath, lying on the floor among *Lindy*'s ruins—seeing himself in duplicate beside Jillan and Paul—"O God," he said, third of his kind, and gathering himself shakily to his feet, stood dazed in the shock of too many changes, far too fast.

"Damn you," his brighter image shouted, and he thought he was intended, that the outrage was aimed at him.

"Damn you," Rafe shouted at the walls, "—Kepta!"

"He's real," said Rafe Two. "Don't frighten him worse than he is."

Another duplication happened, another Jillan, another Paul, wide-eyed and terrified, who confronted their startled selves in voiceless shock.

"What are you up to?" Rafe screamed, himself, original, fists clenched. "Kepta—*They're not toys! They're alive, you hear me, Kepta? They don't just turn off. It's not a bloody game! Stop—stop it, hear?"*

There was riot among the passengers. *"Stop!"* <^> wailed. "Stop, stop, stop—"

<> did more than that. The pulse went through the ship in no uncertain strength.

Paul One flinched, dropped his tormenting of the Rafe-simulacrum and turned fierce attention toward the duplicates and the corridor <> protected.

"Diversions," said </>. "Don't regard them. <> means to lure you into reach."

"I know," Paul said, having gotten *I* back wider than it had been. *I* was wide as all the universe. *I* was unstoppable, having tendrils in Rafe-shape, and in his own; and extensions into < / >. He pulled at another memory, warped it out of shape, and Rafe-mind writhed in agony.

< / > gained another section of the ship by complete default, for = = = = realigned = = = =self: the Cannibal had ambitions, and < >'s indirection and < / >'s aggressiveness advised = = = = which allegiance was, at the moment, the better choice.

< > sent out another pulse which resounded painfully through the ship.

But it did not deter desertions.

There was silence, dreadful silence, among *Lindy*'s ruin. Rafe recovered himself, wiped at his eyes, ashamed of the terror he had created. He was *theirs,* in common, their stability, the one thing impossible to counterfeit. He sensed their dependency. He sniffed, unheroically wiped his nose, sat down in the command chair and wiped his eyes again. None of them could touch him, none lay the least substance of a comforting finger on him, his sad-faced, devoted ghosts. They only waited in a half-ring about the console, two of everyone, even of himself.

"I'm sorry," he said to them. "Really sorry." Another wipe at his eyes with the heel of his hand.

"That's all right," said one of his doppelgangers—he did not even know which one. They had a right to be ashamed, he thought; and upset; and they looked to be.

"Someone want to fill me in?" the other of his doppelgangers said. "I'm lost. I think several of us are. I think—" with a frightened glance at the one transparent as himself: "I was here; and talked to Rafe— about leaving the ship. Then it got me—in the dark. Am I far off? How lost am I?"

"Hours," Rafe said, himself. "No farther."

"You're still hoarse."

"Yes," he said, looking at the two Jillans. He could not tell them apart. There was no difference. That, more than anything, hurt him. He wanted there to be a difference. He wanted one to be real, an original, his sister; and there were two, both hurting, both claiming the right to existence and to him.

"We're all right," said the leftmost Paul, who had the rightmost's steadying hand on his shoulder. The speaker's voice was thin. "We understand. I think we've got the drill down pat. It's just the shock. . . ."

"Dammit," said Rafe One. He stood up, holding out empty, helpless hands, to him, to the Jillan-newcomer. "I'm sorry. I'm sorry, hear."

"I know," said Rafe Three. "It's what he says—the shock of it. Waking up—finding we're not . . . what we were prepared to be."

"But we are," said one of the Jillans. The other's mouth was set hard; this one had Jillan's most brittle look, don't-touch-me, don't-pity-me. "It's what I said. We never know—we never know, after a copy's made—which one we are."

"Shut up," the other Jillan said.

"You don't need me," said Jillan (he was sure now) One. The chin firmed, the head lifted. "I'm not your *self*. Stop thinking of me that way."

"Sister," Rafe said, to comfort Jillan. Both faces looked his way, instinctively, and the horror overwhelmed him.

"I didn't plan—" Rafe Three said in his default. "I didn't plan to be superfluous. Wasn't that the word I just used of you? How many of us does it need, for God's sake?" He walked off from them, through *Lindy*'s console. Rafe winced, knowing the self-torment behind that move. "It could get real crowded here," Rafe Three said, recovering his humor, a desperate look back at all the surplus of them, a look upward as something went howling through the speakers overhead. *"Damn that thing!"* And then, with a futile reach at the com controls: *"Com light's on*—Rafe, Rafe—for God's sake, I can't touch it—"

Rafe moved, dived through the simulacrum, pushed the button; but the light went out under his hands and the sound was gone.

"Games," he said. "Dammit, it's playing games with us!"

"((()))!" < > shouted at the culprit, but ((())) ran, evaded a wandering segment of = = = = and kept screaming.

"Lonely," ((())) said when ((())) had stopped eventually. This was improvement of a kind. ((())) had acquired an opinion after eons of raving lunacy. ((())) peered from behind a weak barrier ((())) had erected and looked doubtfully at < >.

"Away!" < > raged at ((())). "Get out of here!"

((())) drew ((())self up on all ((()))'s legs and dropped the barrier. "((())) remember," ((())) said, *"flesh—"*

And that word whispered through the ship with a multitude of connotations as ((())) fled.

<^> leapt out of ((()))'s path and shuddered, coming close to < >.

"Why haven't <^> deserted too?" < > wondered.

"Bravery," said <^>.

"I was the last it copied," Paul said, in the silence, in the devastation of them all. "I think—I think I know things. I think my double understands best what's going on. I was the last it took." He walked over to the counter, settled on the edge in a parody of sitting, for it was hard to recall after a lifetime of having a body that it made little difference where it rested, except it put him near the one of them that could occupy a seat and make its fabric give. Rafe looked at him— bruised, shadow-eyed. Rafe Two stood godlike in his handsomeness; Three had a foredoomed look, brooding and quiet. And Jillan, his Jillan, was the image of her brothers, her face so much like theirs and so much more delicate, so doubly resolute, in both her shapes. His own doppelganger came to settle at his side—*so tired he looks,* Paul thought, shocked at himself. He drew an unneeded breath, straightened his shoulders, looked once and achingly at Jillan.

"Kepta and I," he said, "had a real frank talk. I don't know all it expects of me. I suspected it might lie, in several ways. Eventually I— had another impression. That Kepta's got a problem and he's scared. I don't know what he's up to now."

"Do you know more than I do?" his doppelganger asked him.

"No," he said. "More than that, no. God help us."

"God help us," it echoed. "Both."

"What's it want?" one of the Rafe-doubles asked. Three, Paul thought. "I wish someone could bring me up to date."

"There's one of me," Paul said quietly, "my first version, Kepta said. Said he's got some kind of enemy—Kepta has. And that other version of me is on that enemy's side and crazy as they come. Maybe I know how. But that's all I know—" he said to Rafe, slid a glance at Rafe Three. That Rafe was afraid—he saw it, and felt a dim, ugly affirmation of himself.

My darker side, he thought, because it gave him, deeply, secretly— satisfaction. *Rival.* He seized on that idea, refused to let it go until he had turned all sides of it to the light. *Because I'm not strong, and he is. And Jillan is.* He lifted his head and looked at the Original.

"Barriers," he said. "Barriers, Rafe. Jillan—I love you two, you and Rafe. That's the one thing I have to keep telling myself over and over. Kepta said I have to figure out why I love you. And now that I do try to figure it out it's very simple. I'm not a good man without that."

"That's nonsense," Jillan said.

"Oh, but it's not. Without someone to trust I'm not trustable myself. I work on reciprocities. You provide me—environment. You're my morality. And if you fail me I'm worse than lost. You get my other side. Or it gets me. There's a part of me wants more than anything to be like you, independent. Capable. There's a part of me wants to prove you're not capable at all; wants to see you're like me, in need of props and braces. Wants to—affirm my own humanity, I guess, by proving you're like me—Don't say anything," he said to Jillan, because she began to protest the mandatory, affirming things. "You've never seen my insides. I think you needed me, all right. Needed my station credit, someone to work with you, another strong back; my—friendship. I believe that. I really do. You and Rafe. I don't think you really have the least idea what I wanted when I dragged a merchanter into marrying. It was that kind of thing. Affirmation. Environment. Something to define *me* and give me the props I need."

"You're not like that," Jillan said. *His* Jillan, the older one. "That isn't why I married you."

He looked at her, smiled sadly at loyalty reflected in both her versions. "But I am," he said. "That's what you got, Jillan-love. A bad man who's told you the truth for once, because he had to tell it to himself." He gathered himself to his feet and walked off from them, their eyes. Looked back again, having remembered suffering beside Jillan's and his own. "Kepta said a lot would rest on me; and knowing me," he said to Rafe Three, "Kepta judged I needed help. Maybe that's why you're here. I don't know. You're stronger than I am. I need you." And having admitted that: "I'm full of shadow-spots. He said you had only one secret. I won't ask you what that is."

"I have a thousand," said Rafe Three in uncomfortable charity. "Doesn't any human born?"

"You have one," Paul said.

"Damn that thing!" Jillan cried, leaping to her feet. "It's got no bloody right to mess with us!"

"And you," Paul said, staring at her directly, *"use* yours."

Her eyes fixed on him in sudden, white-edged shock. "He told you? He told you that?"

"Not what it was. Just how you work."

"What does it know about humanity?"

He listened to that. Secrets wielded like a shield, deflecting questions that could go through to the heart. He nodded, quite calm about it, armored in the truth. "Trust isn't the way you work. You never trusted me with the truth. Maybe I couldn't have stood it. You always protected me."

"What's that supposed to mean? You're not making sense, Paul."

"You are. Making sense, I mean. To me. Don't change. I love you. Love me back. That's all I want. Does it cost too much?"

"No," she said, not understanding him. She would not, he thought, understand him; or believe truth when she heard it, though she was wise in other ways. And in the wickedness of his heart he found that he was in one way stronger, and wiser, and for once he had something to give away.

He smiled at her. Watched both her versions frown.

"Rafe," he said, looking back at the Original, "I figure when the stuff starts to go, hard, you know?—we'll be separate. Could be any minute. Maybe when we figure something essential Kepta wants he'll snatch us out of here. I want you to know—you're brother, father, mother to me. *She,* my real family—they made her mother in a lab; she and gran did the best they could with me. Ma wasn't any rebel like I told you. They shot her by accident. She just got in the way. That was the way she was. Like gran. Wrong place. Wrong time. That's all."

"Guessed she wasn't any rebel," Rafe said in the faintest, most diffident of voices. "They gave you that station share. They never would have, if she'd been on the rebel side. However young you were."

He nodded, head up, discovering the nakedness he had always suspected with them. "Couldn't impress you, could I?"

"Didn't have to," Rafe said. "Not that way. You're *family,* Paul."

"Family," he said back. "Yes, you are. All the love and hate and everything that is. Everything that holds me together. I want you to know that."

He felt a hand slide past the hollow of his arm, his own Jillan's slim, smooth touch; her head pressed against him.

And beside the counter, the other two, the new-made set, not touching, nonparticipant and already alive, because they had chosen not to touch, because they had not consented to what he felt. He put his arm about his Jillan. At last his doppelganger did, for whatever his own thoughts were—put his about the other Jillan, who drew a deep, insubstantial breath for hers.

"It said," said that other Jillan, "that *two* of you went wrong."

"One of me," said Rafe.

"Or me," said Rafe Two, moving finally, to sit on the counter edge. "We don't really know which one."

"Does it make a difference?" Rafe One asked.

"As to how far off it is," said Rafe Two, "as to how it adapts to the dark—it might."

The Original shook his head. "No. If it came from as early as I think it might—no difference, except in what it's been through."

"Isn't that always the difference?" Paul asked, discovering this in himself. "Events change us. Isn't that why we all exist? I'm not that other Paul. He's not me. We're all of us—very real."

"I feel that way," Rafe Three said with a small, desperate laugh. "I *feel* alive." And looking distractedly at Jillan: "You said that once."

So < > had made < >'s move. </> was not impressed.

"Mistake," </> said, and unleashed the entity </> had made, Paul-Rafe, while </> stalked larger quarry.

"See," <˄> wailed, knowing this, skipping along at < >'s side as they proceeded elsewhere in the ship. "< > have *lost.*"

"Not yet," < > said.

<˄> remained puzzled; and angry. And frightened, that foremost, as < > and <˄> built barriers.

"This is retreat," <˄> said.

"Maneuver," said < >.

"It's late for that," said <˄>.

"Everything is late," < > said.

"< >," < > heard, a pulse that made < > wince. </> had gathered strength. "< >, </> am waiting for < > to cross the line."

Meanwhile Paul One had moved, slipping through the corridors. = = = = went at Paul One's side, in all = = = ='s segments. Some of them shrieked in protest, but they all went, having no choice in this new alignment.

There was dark in the side-corridors of Fargone docks, the kind of deep twilight of betweentimes, between main and alterday, and someone stalked. Rafe ran, in starkest terror.

"Hey, miner-brat," security yelled and he ought to have turned and faced the man, but he had no pass to be across the lines at this hour, a miner in spacer territory.

He rounded a corner, slid in among shipping canisters awaiting the mover to pick them up. Their shadows passed and his heart crashed against his ribs in regular, aching pulses.

They searched. If they caught him they hauled him in for questions; questions led to Welfare, and Welfare to assigned jobs. Forever.

"Please," they would ask of spacers, shyly on the docks, asked them daily, nightly, in the shadows of twilight hours, "sir, got a fetch-carry? Just a chit or two?"

Most had no job for them. Some trusted Jillan but not him. Docksiders stole. Now and again one gave him a message to run—payment at the other end. Sometimes he was cheated. Once a white-haired woman offered him money and a bed and he took the key she offered and went to that sleepover, humiliated when he discovered what she had not wanted at all. Just charity, for a starving kid trying to stay off Station Welfare lists.

He was humiliated more that he had been willing to sell himself, for what she gave away.

And he did not tell Jillan about that night. He did not tell it even to Paul.

"The time has come," < > said, and made two simulacra. "Wear this," < > said to <ʌ> of Jillan-shape. "<ʌ>'ll find things in common with her."

"I don't know what to do," Paul said to Rafe's question. "I don't—"

And there were two more of them: a fourth Rafe; a third Jillan standing there, in front of the EVApod that reflected them and the hall askew in its warped faceplate.

A pair of them, with that deep-eyed stare. There was horror in newcomer-Jillan's eyes.

"Kepta," Paul said, guessing.

And: "Kepta," said Rafe, getting to his feet as the rest of them had, "dammit, let Jillan be!"

"Call him Marandu," Kepta said of the anxious Jillan-shape beside him. "That was something like his name. *He* doesn't quite describe him. But *she* doesn't do it either."

"More games."

"No," Kepta said. "Not now." Jillan/Marandu had hold of Rafe/Kepta's arm. Kepta shook off the grip and walked aside with a glance upward and about as if his sight went beyond the walls. "It's quiet out there now. It won't be for long. It's moving slowly, expecting traps."

"What are you here for?" asked Jillan One.

"You," Kepta said, and turned a glance at Paul. "It's time."

"Leave Jillan here," Paul said.

"Which one?" it asked him, and sent a chill through his blood. It faced him fully. "You choose. A set of you will stay here safe. A set of you will face it. Likely the encounter will ruin that set. Which?"

"*None* of them," Rafe said. "Leave them alone."

"*It* won't," Kepta said, and looked back at Paul. "I sent a full set here—to keep the promise; I brought them early so that they would have some contact with the oldest. Continuity. That's as much as I could give. Now it's time, and no time left. Four to stay and three to go. Shall I choose? Have you not discovered difference?"

"I'll go," Paul said. He cast a look at his doppelganger, poor bewildered self, standing there with its mouth open to say something. "No," it protested. *"No.* It's why I was born, isn't it?"

Then things seemed clear to him, clear as nothing but Jillan had ever been. "Take Jillan and Rafe of the new set," he said, "and me, of the old." He looked straight at his doppelganger as he said it, proud of himself for once. "I know what the score is."

And the dark closed about him.

"No!" he heard Rafe's hoarse shout pursuing them. He felt a hand seek his in the dark—Jillan's. Felt her press it hard. He trusted it was the latest one, as he had asked. "You did the right thing," Rafe Three said—unmistakably Rafe, clear-eyed and sensible, as if he had drawn his first free breath out of the bewilderment the others posed. "What now?"—for Rafe was not senior of this group.

They were gone, just gone, and there was silence after. Rafe stood helpless between Rafe Two and Jillan; and Paul's hours-younger self, his substitute, whose look at Jillan was apology and shame.

She just stared at that newborn Paul, with that dead cold face that was always Jillan's answer to painful truths.

"What's happening out there?" Rafe Two asked. "What's *happening?*"

"War," said that Paul, in a faint, thin voice. "Something like. That Paul that changed—it wants the rest of us. And he's got to stop it. Paul has to. The real one. The one I belong to. The one I *am.*"

"It can make more of us," Jillan said. "It can keep this thing going —indefinitely."

"It won't," Paul Three said. "It won't take the chance. It said it wouldn't risk the ship. Kepta's words."

"It—" Jillan said; and: "O *God!"*—her eyes directed toward the tunnel-length.

Rafe spun and looked, finding nothing but dark; and then the howling sound raced through the speakers, leaving them shivering in its wake.

$</>$ made haste now, sending tendrils of $</>$ self into essential controls. $</>$ encountered elements of $<>$, which $</>$ had expected, but $<>$'s holdouts were growing few. There had been major failures. $<>$'s resistance collapsed in some areas, continued irrationally in others.

Other passengers, such as |:|, declared neutrality and retreated to the peripheries.

Paul, meanwhile. . . . $</>$ wielded Paul/Rafe like an extension of $</>$ self.

The variant minds of the simulacra were the gateway, $</>$ reckoned. < > had invested very much of < >self in the intruders, which had proved, in their own way, dangerous.

The passengers were mobilized, as they had not been in eons. There was vast discontent.

"< > has lost < >'s grip," </> whispered through the passages, everywhere. "< > has been disorganized. </> am taking over. Step aside. Neutrality is all </> ask—until matters are rectified."

"Home," said one of [], with the ferocity of desire. [] forgot that []'s war was very long ago, or that []'s species no longer existed, and whose fault that was. But they were all, in some ways, mad.

Kepta joined them, a Rafe-shape with infinity in its eyes. It stood before them in the featureless dark, and Paul faced it in a kind of numbness which said the worst was still coming; and soon.

He was, for himself, he thought, remarkably unafraid; not brave— just self-deprived of alternatives.

"It will be there," Kepta said, turning and pointing to the dark that was like all other dark about them. "Distance here is a function of many things. It can arrive here very quickly when it wants."

"What's it waiting for?"

"My extinction," Kepta said, "and that's become possible. You must meet it on its own terms. You must stand together, by whatever means you can. You will know what to do when you see it, or if you don't, you were bound to fail from the beginning; and I will destroy you then. It will be a kindness. Trust me for that."

And it was gone, leaving them alone; but a star shone in the dark, a murkish fitful thing. Rafe pointed to it; Paul had seen it already.

"Is that it?" Rafe wondered.

"I suppose," said Paul, "that there's nothing else for it to be."

"Make it come to us," Jillan said. "Get it away from whatever allies it has."

"And what if its allies come with it?" Paul asked. "No. Come on. Time—may not be on our side."

They advanced then. And it moved along their horizon, a baleful yellow light.

Chapter Nine

They waited; that was what they were left to do, prisoners of the corridor, of *Lindy*'s scattered pieces, of Kepta's motives and the small remnant of former realities.

"I can't," Rafe Two mourned, having tried to will himself away into the dark where Paul had gone; and Rafe himself looked with pity on his doppelganger.

"That'll be Kepta's doing," Jillan said. She sat tucked up in a chair that phased with her imperfectly, near Paul, loyally near their relict Paul, whose face mirrored profoundest shame.

"I tried too," Paul Three said, in a hushed, aching tone, as if he were embarrassed even to admit the attempt. "Nothing. It's shut down, whatever faculty we had."

"You were outmaneuvered," Rafe said. "He's a little older than you."

"Not much," Jillan said to Paul on her own. "Hours. But a few choices older. He *knew*, that's what. He'd had time to figure it out; and he was way ahead of us. He got us all."

There was a glimmering of something in Paul Three's eyes. Resolve, Rafe thought. Gratitude. And something he had suddenly seen in that other Paul Gaines, the look of a man who knew absolutely what he was doing.

Rafe Two picked that up, perhaps. Perhaps envied it; their minds were very close. That Rafe got up and turned his back as if he could not bear that confidence.

Why not me? The thought broadcast itself from Rafe Two's every move and shift of shoulders. He walked away, partly down the corridor. *Why not choose me? I was best. Oldest. Strongest.*

Responsibility.

"Don't," Rafe said. "Stay put."

"I am," Rafe Two said, facing him against the dark, with bitterness. "I can't blamed well get anywhere down the hall, can I?"

And then there was a Jillan-shape at his back, glowing in the dark.

"Rafe," Rafe said, and Rafe Two saw his face, their faces, if not what was at his back. Rafe Two acquired a frightened look and turned to see what had appeared behind him in the corridor.

The light retreated before them, continually retreated.

"I guess," Rafe said, not breathing hard, because they could not be out of breath, or tired, nor could what they pursued, "—I guess it's not willing to be caught."

"If that's the case," said Jillan, "we don't have a prayer of taking it."

"Unless it's willing to catch us," Paul said. "Maybe it's counted the odds and doesn't like three of us at once. *I'll* go forward. Maybe that will interest it."

"You can bet it will," Jillan said, and caught his arm. She was strong; strong as he: that was the law of this place; and he was going nowhere, not against her, not by any means against the two of them. Rafe stepped in his way and faced that distant light in his stead.

"You!" Rafe yelled at it. "Lost your nerve? Never had it in the first place?"

"That's one way," Paul said. "Let me tell you about that thing. It knows it's a coward. It lives with that real well. It knows all kinds of things about itself. That's its strength."

"You're wrong," Jillan said. "If it's you it's not a coward."

"Let's say it's prudent," he said. "Let's say—it knows how to survive. If we split up—it'll go for one of us. Me, I'm betting."

"Me," said Jillan. "I'm the one it doesn't have."

"It's scared of you," Paul said with a dangerous twinge of shame. "I really think it is."

"What's *that* mean?" Jillan asked.

"That. Just that. It is. Keep pressing at it." He walked farther with them. The light they pursued grew no brighter.

"Ever occur to you," Jillan asked then, "that we're being lured—ourselves?"

"*Where's Kepta?*" Rafe demanded of the uncounseling dark, the void about them. "Dammit, where is he? He could be more help. What's he expect of us?"

"Kepta's saving his own precious behind," Jillan said. "We're the delaying action. Don't you figure that?"

But they kept walking, kept trying, together, since he could not persuade them otherwise. "Think of something," Paul said. "That's *me* we're chasing. It knows every move I'd make. Think of something to surprise it."

"It knows us," Jillan said, a low enthusiastic voice. "Too bloody well. It's not taking the bait."

"Kepta?" Rafe Two asked, facing Jillan's shape that strode toward him; but even while he asked it he kept backing up until he was within *Lindy*'s limits, until he had Rafe beside him, and true-Jillan and Paul Three. There was something very wrong with that Jillan-shape, something very much different from Kepta in its silence, the curious unsteadiness of its walking.

"Kepta?" Rafe himself asked it, at his side, half-merged with him.

"Maranduuuu," it said, this puppetlike Jillan-shape, "*Marand-u, I—*"

"Stay back from us." Rafe Two held out a forbidding hand, making himself the barrier, remembering in a cold sweat that it could touch him, if not the original, that he could grapple with it if he had to—but he had wrestled Jillan-shape before when it was Kepta and he knew his chances against that strength. "Keep your distance. Jillan, Paul, get Rafe back. Get him back!"

"Safe," it said. Its hands were before it, a humanlike gesture that turned into one chillingly not, that tuck of both hands against Jillan's naked breasts, like the paws of some animal. One hand gestured limply. "Safe. Kepta sent—" Eyes blinked, as if it were sorting rapidly. *"Me,"* it decided. "Me. Marandu. To defend you."

"Do your defending from there," Rafe Two said, hand still held out, as if that could stop it.

< / > invaded another center of the ship, dislodging a few of the simpler passengers, who wept; and one complex, ||||, who sent out a strong warning pulse.

< / > did not counter this, or attack. The entity was not capable of aggression, but of painful defense. < / > offered |||| choices. In time |||| redefined the necessities of ||||'s situation and wandered away.

That was the first layer of < >'s defense about the replication apparatus. It went altogether too quickly, tempting < / > to imprudent advance on the chiefest prize: the inner circle, the computer's very heart.

So < / > guessed where < > had centered < >self: < / > would have done so. < > was there, wound about the replication apparatus and possessing every template there was. It was necessary to advance against that center sooner than < / > had intended, and < / > knew raw terror, approaching this place.

There were doomsday actions that < > could take.

"< / > advise < > against such measures," < / > said from a safe distance to the core. "They are ultimately destructive. Surplus copies of ——" (< / > used a pronoun collective of the ship and passengers) "would complicate matters. Get out of there. Give up. < / > promise < / > will replicate < > when < / > have won the ship, when things are secure."

And in < >'s infuriating silence:

"< >," < / > said, "have < / > not always kept the promises < / > make?"

"Are not < / > one that < > kept?" came the answer, faint and deceptively far away. "< > regenerated < / > in our last such impasse. < > did as < > said. Give up," < > added, a hubris that astonished < / >, "and < > will show < / > this mercy one more time. The struggle is inconclusive again. There *is,*" < > added further, "always another time."

</> laughed in outrage. "</> will amalgamate these newcomers with <> when </> copy <>, since <> are so defensive of them. </> will add <.> and lump all </>y enemies together."

"Do this," <> whispered, no louder than the whisper of the stars against the ship-sensors, loud as the universe, "do this and regret it infinitely. Reciprocation, </>. Remember that. </> don't have the keys <> have. </> always have to resurrect <>. <>'ve changed the keys; <>'ve been doing it all through <>y waking. <> learned—from </>ur old trick."

This was likely truth. <> was fully capable of altering the ship. But </> disdained the warnings and pressed forward, urging </>'s other parts to advance as well.

Paul/Rafe was one. He was afraid, in aggregate. He trembled, constantly keeping his enemy in sight, but constantly assailed with doubts.

He was in space, the stars about him, nothing for reference.

He looked about for Lindy, *but there was nothing there.*

So Rafe-mind fought him still, deep within his structure, having saved back some shred of itself for this. It fed Paul self-doubts.

Fargone station's deepest ways, and it was not Security after Rafe Murray this time; it was another kind of force.

No one freelance-smuggled with the likes of Icarus, *no one crossed the moneyed interests that ran what they liked past customs; and if they caught him, if they saw his face—*

So Paul fought back, and drove Rafe-mind into shuddering retreat.

Rafe made a mistake, a wrong turn in docks he had known all his life; but a stack of canisters against the wall became a maze, became a dead end, and cut off his retreat.

"Got you, you bastard," said the first of the four that filled the aisle between the towering cans.

He did not defend himself. It was not wise to antagonize them further. He only flung up his hands and twisted to shield himself as best he could, let them beat him senseless in the hopes they would be content with that, private law privately enforced, the kind they might not want Fargone authority involved in.

They did a thorough job. They knew, from his lack of defense or outcry, that he would not be going to authorities to make complaint;

that he had something to lose that way more than they could do to him. And in that frustration they took their time about it.

"Where's the other one?" they asked him over and over, knowing they had chased two, but he had diverted them his way. He never answered them about Jillan, not a syllable.

That was not the kind of thing Paul had hoped for. The memory died, quickly; but Rafe-mind stayed intact, locked into that moment with deliberate focus, with a certain satisfaction, the same he had shown the smugglers from *Icarus.*

I, Paul kept thinking, until it was himself who had been betrayed and Rafe had done it. So he warped all such memories.

Rafe wept, believing it at last.

No police, he had thought, dragging himself away with a broken arm that, finally, had cost him and Jillan four months' savings for the meds. He evaded the police, passers-by, all help. There were questions that way; there was Welfare always ready to take charge of them and assign them a station job or send them to the mines to pay for Welfare help, forever, no hope of ships, no way out of debt for all their hopeless lives. A broken arm, the other things they did—that was small coin for freedom; and he must not talk, never complain, no matter what they did.

"I fell," he told the meds, three days after, when the arm got beyond their care, and Jillan made him go.

There were inconsistencies. At times he thought that Paul had helped them; at others it seemed that Paul was destitute as they, which he had not remembered.

Rich, always rich, Paul Gaines, superior to him, clean and crisp in his uniform, station militia, sometimes Security—

Was it Security, then? Was it the police and not Icarus *crew that had found him in the corridors, that day and left him bruised and bleeding among the canisters for outbound ships?*

Welfare agents?

Paul?

Things muddled in his mind, defense collapsing.

"Paul," he murmured, and felt the invasion of his mind, the superfluity of limbs which worked against his will.

"They're there," Paul whispered to him. It seemed that he could see the folk of *Icarus* far across the dark. "There they are."

"Crazy," Rafe whispered back; and in a paroxysm of effort: "Paul—you *died.*"

"Good," Paul said, quite satisfied with his state. "They're Icarids, Rafe. Aren't they? Let's go do something about them, why don't we?" The legs moved.

"No," Rafe cried, "no, no, no."

And Paul enjoyed it. It was a weapon, Rafe's fear, and he had mastered it.

They were no nearer than they had ever been on that dark and starless plain, the horizonless void which felt like nothing to their feet. The glow moved steadily, changing angles as they did, as if some invisible line connected it and them.

"It's leading us," Rafe said, glancing aside as he said it; and Paul agreed the same heartfrozen moment that *something* turned up in their midst, all black segmented coils and legs glowing yellow at their joints as if light escaped. It towered among them, in nodding blind movements of its head.

"*Aaaiiii!*" it wailed.

"Get *back,*" Jillan cried, hauling at his arm. "Run, for God's sake, run! Paul! It can't catch us—"

It did. Shock numbed his nonexistent bones, ached in his joints as it roiled into him and out again. "Paul!" Jillan yelled; she and Rafe came back to distract it from him, darting this way and that.

"Help," came a strange multiple voice, choruslike, as it pursued their darting nuisance to it. "Help, help, help—"

"Look out!" Paul cried, for Jillan misjudged: he flung himself at it as Rafe did, as she screamed.

It hit like high voltage: the beast itself yelped and writhed aside. All of them screamed, and then was silence.

Paul froze . . . . in the numbness after shock, the fear that Jillan and Rafe were likewise crippled—all these things applied. Most, it was the voice, the dreadful voice that wailed at them and stole wits with its frightfulness. "Help," it kept saying, and its forward end nodded up and down serpentlike, like something blind. It made a whistling sound. "Rafe? Rafe? *Fles-sh-sh.*"

"O God," Jillan breathed, moving then, tugging backward at their arms. "Get back, hear me—*get back*. It's nothing we can handle, not this thing—"

"Lonely," it said, snuffling; it had the sound of a ventilation system, a periodic sibilance. "F-f-flesh-sh. Rafe—lonely."

"Don't!" Paul cried, for it had encircled them, leaving them nowhere left to run. And to nothing at all, to the betraying, lightless air: *"Kepta! Help!"*

"Can't," it said, snuffled, in its myriad of voices. "Name—can't—*Aaaaiiieee!"*

"It's that howler-thing!" Jillan cried.

"Aaaaaaee," it said. The head swayed back again and aimed toward the dark. "Came to this ship. We. Long time—long—Crazy, some. Rafe-mind ran."

"What, *ran?"* Rafe Three asked it.

"Fight," it said, blind head questing. "Fight." The voices entered unison. "—go with. Fought once. Paul—" The head nodded off toward the star, the glow along the horizon, that seemed nearer now.

"What are you?" Paul asked.

"Fought once," it said, which seemed the sum of its identity. It started off, in pursuit of the ebbing light.

Dead, Paul reminded himself. *You're already dead. Quit worrying. Time's short.* And he wished that death was all.

"Come on," he said to Jillan and Rafe Three, because he saw nothing else to do. He started walking in the wake of the looping creature, which humped and zigged its way through the dark like some great sea creature aswim in the murk, with graceful fluidity.

Rafe was by him; he never doubted his constancy; and Jillan at his other side, never faltering.

The star grew in their sight.

Worm came circling back to them when the will-o'-the-wisp they chased had begun to shine globular and planetlike in the dark.

"Paul," Worm named that light. "Rafe. Pain."

"Take us there," Rafe Two demanded, of that Jillan-shape that had come to them. "Take us there, you hear me? If you want your enemies fought, then, dammit, let us out of here!"

And the shadow-eyes turned from regarding the wall, came back to them, so full of secrets that a chill stirred all through Rafe's own all-too-substantial bones.

"You," Jillan yelled at Jillan-shape, "answer, will you? Why do you keep us here?"

"For his defense," it said; Jillan/Marandu in a far, soft voice. "For yours."

"Kepta cares," Rafe Two said in heaviest bitterness. "I'm sure."

"For his defense," it said again, making different sense than before.

"For *Kepta's?*" Rafe asked, himself. "Is that the game?"

"Game." The thing stood there with that infinity-look, god/goddesslike in stillness. "That's not what to call it. The ship is at risk. We're all at risk. There are always quarrels. Some would like to sleep. Some find that more comfortable. Time wears—on some. But we go on doing what we were set to do."

"What?" Rafe asked. He stood behind Rafe Two's shoulder, dodged round him to the fore as if he were solid, out of courtesy. "*What* were you set to do? What are you up to?"

"Some passengers never ask," Marandu said. "There's one, for instance, completely without curiosity. It doesn't dream either. But it knows a lot of things. It can't dream because it can't forget. Different approaches to consciousness."

"Stop the nonsense," Jillan snapped at it. "You've got your fingers in my mind right now. You can guess what I'd ask; so answer it."

"Where the others are?" A blink. "But you *don't* know that. You think you're physical. So do they." It cast a disturbed look at Rafe. "You know. Kepta knows you know. You saw the apparatus. You ought to have told them."

A chill like ice came over him, foreknowledge of harm.

"What's it mean?" Rafe Two asked. "Rafe, what's it saying?"

"You don't have physical bodies," Rafe said. He turned his shoulder to the intruder, to look instead at them. "Patterns. Computerlike. *Simulacra.* You're not physical."

"What do you mean?" Jillan asked. "Make sense, Rafe."

"I'm making the best I know."

"We're *here,*" Jillan said.

"Position in the ship," said Jillan/Marandu, "is simultaneous. You only control a small priority. Kepta's, mine—is virtually universal in the circuitry. Size—is illusory; distance is; all these things—are what you choose to manifest. What I choose—in your shape."

"You mean we're bloody *programs?*" Rafe Two cried, and with a wild, despairing look: "Rafe?"

"You're real," Rafe said. "You go on living, changing. You always knew that. Is a separate body so important?"

"Oh, damn," Rafe Two breathed, and shook his head. *"Dammit, twin."*

"Rafe," Paul said fretfully, stepping through the counter. *"He* doesn't know. Paul doesn't know . . . what he's up against out there. They don't know what they are. Marandu—whatever you call yourself —Send me to him. Now. While there's time."

There was doubt in Jillan/Marandu. It showed in the eyes, in the nervous clench of hands to the breast. Indecision.

"Where's Kepta?" Rafe asked, in sudden, horrid certainty. "Marandu, has Kepta—place?"

The head jerked in a faint—perhaps—negation.

"What *is* Kepta, Marandu?"

"I," it said, flinching back, almost fading out. It looked afraid. "I'm one version."

"One?"

"One," it said.

It had grown from globe to legged shape to figure, still coasting along the formless horizon in the dark.

But the legs were many; the reverse-silhouette warned of deformity.

"Steady," Paul told his companions, told himself, for now he truly knew why he had come, that it was his monster; and that in one sense and perhaps both shapes he was to die here, again, and soon. He searched for Rafe's hand, Jillan's, hugged them close; and Worm lurched along beside him.

The light receded then.

"It's running away," Jillan said. "How can it get distance on us, when we can't catch it?"

"Now," said Worm in its multiplicity of voices. *"Fight.* Fight now."

"How?" Paul asked it. He had nerved himself, and now in default, the old weakness came back, the old insecurity, deadly as swallowed glass, and worked within his gut. He should not have taken the lead. He was not up to this. It outmaneuvered him—that easily.

Then he cast a look at Worm, one wild surmise. "Worm—how? How do *you* come and go?"

It knotted upon its coils like a wounded snake, convulsed, phased with them in one aching shock that hit the nerves and fled.

"O *God,*" Rafe moaned, catching his balance where it had thrown him, as it had thrown them all. Jillan gasped and staggered on her feet, and Paul—Paul refused to think of ground or up or down, but absorbed the shock and shuddered.

Homeworld, he thought out of some source like old memories; remembered—a world like orange ice, with skies that melted and ran; with lightnings like faint glow constant in the clouds; and drifters, drifters with no color at all except the backflare of the clouds—*That you?* he whispered to Worm. *Was that you?* But whatever Worm had tried to say was gone.

The nodding head touched him, and now, with the whiskered, chitin-armored head thrust up before him, it arched its body and presented to him the upper surface; five jewels shone atop its head, black and glistening, and he thought of eyes.

"Come," it whispered back, and its bristles quivered. "Passage."

There was difference in the dark, as if something dire had happened, and yet nothing had changed.

Except suddenly, to their left, a figure loomed distinct.

"O God," Jillan said. "It's *moved* us—"—meaning Worm; for they *were* where the enemy was.

Paul stood still, and Rafe did beside him, facing this nightmare, this many-limbed amalgam of themselves, a thing of legs and arms and faces. It turned slowly, presenting Paul-face to them, and it smiled with a gorgon look.

"The thing got you here," Paul One said. "I wonder if it can get you out. What do you think?"

And Rafe-face answered: "*Kill it,* Rafe, kill it, stop it, stop him—"

"Let me hold you," said Paul One, offering its arms; and Worm gibbered: "*No—*"

"What do we do?" Rafe asked, Rafe Three, tight and low, backing up until they made one line with Jillan. "Paul, did it tell you what to do?"

"Worm," Paul said, his gut liquid with fear. "Worm, get us out of here!"

They were elsewhere, at a little greater distance. They hugged one another in shock, trembling. Paul held Jillan; Rafe held them both; and Worm made a circle about them, looping and making small hisses of defiance or consternation.

Lost, Paul thought. *We're lost, we're helpless against that thing.*

And then he remembered Jillan, and took her gold-glowing face between his hands, making her look up at him. "It hasn't got you," he said. "It hasn't got *you,* Jillan. That monster's one short. We're one stronger. You're my difference."

"I can't do it, Paul. *Can't.*"

You must meet it on its own terms, Kepta had said.

You will know what to do when you see it, or if you don't, you were bound to fail. . . .

"There's one way," he said to her, "one way we can meet it all at once, the way it is, on its terms." Jillan looked so much afraid, for once in her life afraid. He wanted to cry for her; wanted to hit out at whatever threatened them, and instead he touched Jillan's face, reminding himself they both were dead and hopeless and illusion only. Rafe had more than he: a living self. And less, far less. "Want you to trust me," he said, "Jillan; want you to do with me—*with* me—what it's done to Rafe. Just slip inside; we're not that substantial: *it* did it. So can we."

There was already contact. She pressed herself against him then, harder and harder. "I can't," she said then. "I *can't.* You're solid to me."

He tried too, from his side. "Rafe," he said, extending his left arm, and Rafe came against them, held them tight with all his strength, but there was no merging.

"Won't work," Jillan said, *"won't."*—And he felt all too much the fool, trying the possible-impossible, the thing that Paul did, that Kepta did as a matter of course. Worm looped about them all, circled, wailing its distress. "Help," It cried. "Help, help—"

Worm.

"Worm—how do you do it? How do you *pass through us? Show us, Worm!"*

"Make," Worm said.

"What—make? Make what?"

It whipped through their substance with one narrowing of its legged coils. Rafe screamed, becoming part of it, and Jillan—

The pain reached him. His vision divided, became circular, different from his own, and he owned many legs—

—view of skies like running paint, lightnings, repeated shocks, the sound of thunders never ceasing—

Fargone swinging in ceaseless revolution; Lindy's *dingy boards; the oncoming toad-shaped craft and the merchanter* John Liles—

Got to destruct, destruct, destruct—All those kids and lives—

A thousand of them, Rafe—

—self-abandonment—

It's dumping!—

Jillan's voice, reprieve, with his finger on the button, the red button that was a ship's last option—

Cool and calm: It's dumping, Paul—

We're here, Rafe said, calmer and calmer now.

We're—wherever we've gotten to. Take it easy, Paul; easy—

The pain had stopped. Worm eased from their body. Their hearing picked up multiple sound from somewhere, like wind rushing; there was—if they opened their eyes—too much sight, though the universe was black; and the knowledge ripped one way and the other like tides, memories viewed from one side and the other, shredded, revised.

—walkwalkwalk—

Some one of the multiple brain chose movement: Rafe, Paul thought; Paul tried to cooperate. There was progress of a kind.

Awkward trifaced thing maneuvering into Paul's way. There was humor in that self-image, even in extremity: that was Rafe-mind, steady and self-amused.

I love you, Paul thought to their amalgamated self over and over again, without reservation, without stint; and got it back, Rafe-flavored. He wanted Jillan too; felt her fear, her reserve against all their wants: it was all too absolute.

Me, she insisted, *me, myself, I, I, I*—even while she moved her limbs in unison with them. There was pain in that.

"We need you," Paul whispered, desperate. He *knew,* of a sudden, knew what privacy in Jillan this union threatened. She shielded them from her own weapons, from rage, from resentment, every violence.

"You're our defense, Jillan; Rafe's our solid core; me—I go for *him* when I can get at him. But I need what you've got—all of it, hear—no secrets, Jillan-love."

"No one needs all," Jillan flung back at them both. "But that was always what you asked."

It stung, it burned. It took them wrathfully inside itself and taught them privacy.

No one, thought Jillan-mind, with a ferocity that numbed, *no one can ask myself of me.*

Our shield, Paul whispered to Rafe, in the belly of this amalgam they had become. *Give way. Give up for now. Let Jillan have her way.*

There was outrage left: memories of Fargone docks, of Welfare and Security.

You asked it. That was Rafe, in self-defense.

I never asked. You made up your own mind what I should be.

His arm was broken. He had never talked. He never would.

There was terror (Jillan now) *in the dark, hiding there, dodging a drunken spacer who had a yen for a fourteen-year-old, a kid without ship name to defend her—she eluded him, hurled invective at him; shook, afterward, for long, stomach-wracking minutes.*

Grandmother had a number (Paul-mind, in self-defense) *which all lab-born had.*

"Why don't I?" he had asked, wanting to be like this tranquil model of his life. He touched the number, fascinated by it. He could see it forever, fading-purple against Gran's pale mine-bleached skin, against frail bones and the raised tracery of veins under silk-soft skin. It was one with the touch of Gran's hand, the softest thing he knew; but she had wielded blasters, shoved rock, had a mechanical leg from a rockfall in the deep. Her eyes, her wonderful eyes, black as all the pits, her mouth seamed and sere and very strong: the number brought back that moment.

"You don't want one," his mother said, harshly, as harshly as she ever spoke to him. "Fool kid, you don't want one of those."

"Your gran's lab-born," a girl had said once, seven and cruel as seven came, the day his gran had died. "Made her in a tank. That's what they did. Bet they made a dozen."

He had cried at the funeral; his mother did, which reassured him of her humanity.

But perhaps, he thought even then, she was pretending.

"None of her damn business," Jillan-mind insisted of that seven-year-old, with a great and cleansing wrath; and Rafe was only sorry, gentler, in his way. "Stupid kid," he said. There was no doubt in them of humanity; the memory grew clean, purged; "She loved you," Rafe-mind said, confusing his own half-forgotten spacer mother with the daughter of lab-born gran. *He* knew; Jillan knew; there was no doubt at all in them, why a woman would work all her life and hardly see her son—to leave him station-share, the sum of all she had, her legacy. Merchanters knew, who had bought a ship with the sum of their own years.

They progressed; limbs began to work.

Rafe's suffering in this—a stray thought from Paul, shame, before the man who was so godlike perfect, feeling his horror at the shambling thing they had become.

Shut up, Jillan said, severe and lacking vanity, as she had killed it in herself years ago (too great a hazard, on the docks, to look better than one had to, to attract anything but, maybe, work. One had to look like business; and be business; and mean business; and she did).

Use what you've got. (Rafe-mind, whose vanity was extreme, and touching, in its sensitivity.)

You can't get pregnant, Jillan hurled at him, ultimate rationality; and caught his longing, his lifelong wish for some woman, for family—

Vanity serves some purposes, Rafe-mind thought, recalling it was his smoothness, his glib facility with words that got them what they had: he had bent and bent, so Jillan never had to—*A room in a sleepover, an old woman gave it to me—I took even that. Even that, for you—*

She felt the wound, shocked. Her anger diversified, became a vast warm thing that lapped them like a sea.

Mine, she thought of them, and saw Paul-shape ahead of them. Wailing went about them. Worm nudged their flanks, little jolts of pain too dim to matter.

"Paul," Worm said, slithering about them, round and round; and the creature before them lingered, murkish in its light. Limbs came and went in it. The face changed constantly.

Chapter Ten

"You're a copy," Rafe said to Marandu/Jillan's faded image.

"Yes," Marandu said. The hands, drawn up to the breast, returned to human pose; Marandu/Jillan grew brighter and more definite, with that unblinking godlike stare.

"Computer-generated," Jillan said in self-despite.

"Or we are the computer," Marandu said, turning those too-wise eyes her way. That stare, once mad, acquired a fearsome sanity. "We're its soft-structure. Its enablement. We're alive individually and collectively. We've been running, and growing, for a hundred thousand years. That's shiptime. Much longer—in your referent. That we're partitioned as we are was accident. It's also kept us sane. It provides us motive. In a hundred thousand years, motive's a very important thing."

"And the enemy," said Paul. "The enemy: what is it?"

"It's Kepta, of course," Marandu said. "It's Kepta Three."

"Be careful," < > said to < >'s counterpart: </> had come very close now, to the center where < > had invested < >self. "You know what < > can do."

At this </> hesitated. "Fool," </> said. "Make another < > and watch it turn on < >. <u></></u> did."

"It was < >y nature then," < > said. "Perhaps < >'ve grown."

"Only older," </> returned, gaining more of < >'s territory. </> extended a filament of </>self all about the center, advanced Paul-mind and = = = = in their attack. The passengers huddled far and afraid, in what recesses they could, excepting ((())), who had forgotten who had killed ((())), long ago; excepting entities like [], who ranged themselves with </>. "< >'ve grown older and less integrated, < >. Give up the center."

"</> are long outmoded," < > said in profoundest disgust. "< > learn; < > change. Come ahead and discover what < > have become."

</> shivered then, in the least small doubt. </> circled and moved back.

"Attack," [] raged, the destroyer of []'s own world. *"Take it!"*

But </> delayed, delayed to think it through in Paul-mind. </> had fallen once before into that trap, < >'s mutability.

Therefore </> used Paul—to learn what < > might have gained from < >'s latest acquisitions; to be certain this time that </>'s strength was equal to the contest. < > *collected* things of late. < > modified < >self in disturbing ways, and was not what < > had been.

</> circled farther back, with more and more agitation, sent out more and more of </>'s allies to scour the perimeters.

"</> want the strangers," </> said. "</> want everything in them."

Hunger was very like that </> felt; and self-doubt; and hate, that too. </> even felt these things in human terms, experimentally.

"This time," < > said, "< > fed </> a warped copy." And suddenly </> doubted whether </>'s theft had indeed been </>'s own idea or half so clever as </> had thought.

</> turned back.

"Where are </> going?" [] howled, ravening at </>'s back. "Coward!"

< > was far from confident. < > huddled in the control center, realizing a serious mistake. < > had, in a taunting lie, revealed too much of </>'s vulnerability; and </> went to solve that problem.

</> had realized the key to </>'s previous defeats.

"Call it a very long time ago," Marandu said, "a very long time ago . . . this ship set out from home. Trade, you might call it; but it's always a mistake to try to translate these things. Call us a probe. Or a sacrifice." The hands drew up again, knotted like prayer beneath the chin; the body drew up in midair and drew toward the floor, legs folding, fetal-like. *"Go. Go . . . go. The—. . . .* There is no word in this brain for that. But that was why. *Life,* you might say. To sample —everything. Exchange. Trade. Commerce . . . of a kind."

"Why?" Jillan insisted to it; "hush," Rafe said, afraid of losing that tenuous truth, of breaking whatever held it to them.

"No translation," Marandu said. "There's never translation of motives; only of acts."

"What happened?" asked Rafe.

A long pause. "An incident. A copy of me existed as precaution. When I died, when the crew did, when the ship was without orders, it activated me."

"Me?"

"I was Kepta then. Division came later."

"What happened then?"

"I kept going. I kept going. Kept transmitting, as long as seemed profitable." Marandu's female mouth jerked. The hands drew up. "Passage of time—negates all motives. Survival is still intact. So is curiosity." Jillan-shape flickered, brightened again and the eyes were set far, far distant. *"Difficulty—"* Marandu said in a voice that moved the lips but scarcely. Sweat glistened on its lip, on its brow beneath the ragged fringe of hair; the legs settled crosswise; hands came down on knees; the shape hovered in midair, naked, dim and glistening with perspiration.

"Marandu," Paul said.

"Difficulty," the voice hissed again.

"Where?" asked Jillan.

"Your duplicates."

"Send me to them," Rafe Two said. *"Let me help them!"*

The eyes which had rolled up came down again and centered. "Kepta is threatened," Marandu said. The sweat rolled in illusory beads. "The enemy has gained a vital point."

"Paul—" Paul said.

"Not yet," Marandu said. The hands were clenched. *"Not yet."*

Rafe clenched his own hands, stared at it in helplessness. "What's it doing? What's Kepta up to?"

"Holding what's essential."

"What's essential?" he flung back at it, but it answered nothing, only sat there, pale and drawn. *"Marandu, what's essential?"*

"Controls," Rafe Two said.

"The computer." Rafe turned, empty-handed, pushed himself off from the control panel and ran, ran in desperation down the hall.

"Rafe!" he heard—his doppelganger's voice.

"Rafe!" Jillan's or Jillan/Marandu's; and a shape leapt into being beside him, a running ghost—Paul, racing along by him in a confused blur of light. Jillan was there, or Marandu; and his doppelganger, half-merged with him.

"Where are you going?" Jillan cried.

"Controls," Rafe gasped, springing perilously from lump to hump of the uneven floor. *"That's* where it has to be, what it has to have—I've been there. I know—"

The knives, he was thinking as he ran, remembering that he was flesh, remembering the arms and blades in that center of the ship. *O God, the knives—*

Station dock; manifests—Lindy *got on toward her loading with* Rightwise *and a Fargone agent wanted to make a fuss, small, dim man with a notepad, a checklist, suspicions.*

"Where's your form B-6878?" he asked.

Rafe searched, desperately, through the sheaf of authorizations.

The clock ticked away, meaning money, each second that loader was engaged. Money and life. All their years had bought—

"Careful," Paul Two said, "careful—" for they had come very near that misshapen thing. Worm hovered round them, and Paul-shape shambled, sidling round them in a green-gold glow that spread along the horizon.

"—is there," Worm whistle-moaned at their backs. *"Danger-dan-ger-danger!"*

"Look!" Rafe cried; and their conjoined, rotating sight discovered a new glow at the opposite side, a thing like Worm, but more horrible, whose white-glowing segments were interspersed with lumps and legged things. Some of them had mouths and others, eyes.

"Eater," Worm gibbered. "Can-Can-Cannibal."

"Come ahead," Paul-voice taunted them from the other side, a god-voice, Paul's deeper tones underlain with Rafe's.

"Fight," howled Worm, hovering behind them. "Coward," it sobbed to itself, over and over again, in half its voices.

Paul One flickered nearer and nearer, growing incrementally in their sight. He opened his/their arms. "Rafe," it said. "Jillan."

"Run," Rafe-voice screamed within it. "Run—!"

"Come on," Paul-mind challenged that shambling thing. He stood firm. Jillan braced herself. "You've caught me; now take me in."

"Look out!" Worm cried; and it was Rafe-mind turned them quick enough: the Cannibal-horror rushed past them in flank attack as the amalgam struck from the other side.

"—an accident," the Welfare man said, "—in the belt. . . ."

"Shut up!" Jillan cried, had cried that day, before he could say the words. Eight years old—she knew, knew what Welfare came to say—

But: "Brother," Rafe Three said, meaning his battered other self, that thing that hung in rags from the monster's side. "O brother—" with the stinging salt of tears.

And Paul: *"Listen to me—"* he told his twisted self, with sorrow that gathered up Jillan-mind and Rafe and all. "Oh, no. You've got it wrong, my friend."

Ugliness flowed back. His own darkness, like a wave: his desire to hurt—

—Rafe wept and begged. He savored that, felt a thrill of sex—

"That's me," Paul said, accepting it, treading on his pride, stripping off all the coverings, revealing all the darks. "Don't be shocked, Jillan; I did warn you, I told you the best I knew—don't leave me, Rafe. Don't. O God, don't—break—"

Paul One writhed; sought Jillan-mind with its hate; sought Rafe. *Kill,* it raged. *Have you—all—all—all—*

It was too much; too strong; too mad. "No!" Rafe pulled them back, dodged aside, for the Cannibal loomed up: *"Back!"* Worm shrieked, and plunged between, tangled its black body with that pale one.

"Worm!" Rafe cried, and Paul dodged again as Worm came flooding back from the Cannibal's assault. Worm's substance was in ribbons. It was missing legs in great patches all down its length; it limped and moaned. But the Cannibal ran, wounded too, ran until it met a thing which took shape out of the dark, a Devourer far larger than itself.

"Paul," that thing said, in a voice far too small and human for its size. Cannibal merged with it; it looped closer to gather Paul One's misshapenness against its glowing side.

"There," it said, contentedly; "there." And lifted up its face to them.

"Rafe—" Paul said. A shudder went through his/their flesh; he felt Jillan's horror: Rafe Three's own dismay.

It was vast. It kept lifting up and up, serpentlike, and the eyes of Rafe-face stared down at them. Beauty—it had that too, Rafe's gone to cold implacability. "I've won," it said; and Paul-Rafe wailed as it sank unwilling into the serpent's glowing side. "There's nothing more to fear."

"No!" Worm wailed. "No, no, no, no—"

"Hush," the whisper thundered. *"Worm*—worm, they call you. Do you know, Worm, what that is? For shame, Paul, to give him a name like that."

"Kepta?" Paul asked. "Is that you?"

"Yes," it said. "Of course I am. Come here."

They reached the great hall, the noded dark. Things gibbered as they ran, voices howled through the overhead, chittered, roared like winds where no winds existed. Rafe kept running, stumbling, fell flat and scrambled up without pause, holding his aching side.

His ghosts stayed with him. Perhaps Marandu was one: he could not tell. There was no light but their bodies, no guidance but their hands that reached impotently to help his weakness. "Where?" Rafe Two asked him, "where now, Rafe?"

"Hallway," he gasped, "third to the left of ours—"

"This way," Rafe Two said, at home in dark, or not truly needing eyes. Rafe gathered himself, sucked a pain-edged breath and ran, staggering with exhaustion.

A Jillan-image materialized in the dark ahead, blazing gold. "Stop!" she/it said. An arm uplifted in a gesture human as the image and as false.

Rafe Two slowed; Rafe ran, experienced nothing but a flare of light and image, stumbled his way on blind in the dark of the passage, reeling from wall to wall. A glow passed him, gave him fitful light, became Jillan before it faded out.

He sprawled, hard, in the shimmer of insubstantial arms that tried to save him; he clawed his way up, sobbing, and kept going. His ghosts were with him again, Jillan, all; they went about him, a glowing curtain, a cloud. He fell again, a third, a fourth time on the hummocks of the floor. He tasted blood, was blind, phosphenes dancing in his eyes.

"Look *out!*" Jillan cried and waved him off, her body out in front of him. He reached out his hands, facing darkness beyond her.

White, sudden light blazed from the ceiling nodes. It lit the room of knives, arms that moved, snicked in unison toward him all attentive, in the lumpish barren plastic of the center he had sought.

"Kepta!" he shouted, backing, for things that gripped and things that cut were still in drifting motion toward him, traveling in extension he had not guessed. *"Kepta!* Stop!"

They kept coming. More unfolded out of recesses of the wall.

"Kepta!"

Jillan-shape materialized there among the knives, flung up arms, opened its mouth and yelled something a human throat did not well stand.

Knives stopped then, frozen in mid-extension, a forest of metal, perilous limbs in which Jillan-shape stood immaterial.

Rafe stood shivering, perceived a dance of light as his own ghosts hovered round him as close as they could get, demolishing themselves on his solidity and reforming.

"Tell Kepta I want to talk with him," Rafe said.

"Kepta won't," Marandu said. His female hands tucked up again like paws. "Go *back.*"

"Because I'm substance? Because I'm alive, with hands to touch this place?"

"Substance," said Marandu among the knives, "is dealt with here."

"Rafe," Paul pleaded with him. "Rafe—*stay alive.* Get out of here."

"It's threatened," Rafe said. He was shivering. They could not feel as much, but the shivers ran through his limbs. *O God. It's going to hurt*—"I'm standing here, Kepta—hear me? I'm not moving. I'm not going to move."

"Kepta advises you," Marandu said—and Marandu's eyes were far-focused, vague and full of dark—"advises you—"

The thing loomed up serpentlike, seductive in its implacability, the serenity of Rafe-face become unassailable and vast.

"Lie," Worm cried, and writhed and looped its wounded coils aside. "Lie, lie—"

"Are you lying?" (Paul.)

"Examine me," it said, this thing with Kepta's name. It extruded a shape from its side, the agglomeration of Paul One. Paul One wailed, writhed as Worm had done. A glowing coil materialized and took it in again. "Come close. See me as I am."

"Go to hell," said Jillan Murray-Gaines, through the amalgam of their lips. "Or are you already in residence?"

"Humor," it said. "Hell. Yes." It laughed, gentle as a breath. "I appreciate the reference. So would the passengers. I'm Kepta. There are dozens of us. We create one another—in endless cycles." It slid closer, and it seemed dangerous to move at all now; but Rafe-mind did, veteran of the docks. They slipped backward together.

"Do you understand?" it asked again. (Another gliding move. Rafe-mind moved them back, but not far enough. It gained.) "Dangerous," it said, "to move without looking. Where's Cannibal? Where's Worm? Are you sure?"

"Don't look," Paul whispered, shivering in their heart. "Don't be tricked."

"You've been ill-advised," Rafe-voice urged, smooth, so very smooth. "Even death—can be remedied. Your copies are exact, down to the very spin of your particles. Your cellular information. Would you be reconstituted? I can do that much."

Paul caught the breath he did not have, felt limbs that were not real —instincts yearned after life and breath, after humanity—

"No," Rafe said. Just—*no,* unreasoning, suspicious. He was twelve again, dockside; the hand held out the coin, too large a coin for simple charity. . . . *No*—from Jillan-mind, brittle-hard, plotting how to run. *Nothing's free; not from this thing—*

"Look out!" cried Paul.

The serpent-shape was quicker. Its vast body slammed down in front of them, turning about them, surrounding them with its coils.

"You just lost your chance," it said.

"Lost," Marandu whispered, fading. "They've failed."

"Let me go to them!" Paul cried. "Let me try!"

"Against a Kepta-form?" Marandu drew itself away, retreating in its dimness. And then it stopped, turned, gazing at them with Jillan's calm face. "Bravery. Yes. I know."

It shimmered out.

"Paul!" Rafe cried.

Then all his ghosts were gone.

Marandu with them. And the lights went out.

Disaster. $<$ $>$ had felt it, not unanticipated. $<$ $>$ felt $<$^$>$'s fear. It shivered through that portion of $<$^$>$self that remained partitioned outside Jillan-shape. There was irony in this: Jillan-mind was darkly stubborn and $<$^$>$ was trapped in that fierceness.

$<$/$>$ discovered that too. Discovered other things.

"O God," Rafe Two murmured, arrived on that darkling plain. "What *is* that thing?"

"The others called it Worm," Marandu said.

It came snuffling and limping toward them, tattered and missing legs among its segments. "Run," it called to them multi-voice; and in other voices: "Fight."

Then they saw the other thing, a thousand times its size.

"My friends," it saluted them like thunder, rearing up to stare down at them with Rafe's haggard face.

"Friends, hell," Jillan said.

"It will take you," Marandu said, a faint and fading voice.

"Damn you," Rafe yelled at Marandu, snatched to hold it by the arm. "Don't leave us—"

Marandu steadied, grew brighter then. "I'm very old," it said, as if that were some grounds for its desertion. "Oldest of all but one."

"So fight it," Jillan said. "Where's your guts?"

And Paul: "Help us. We don't know what to do."

There was silence. The serpent-glow flowed closer. It had Rafe's voice, a whisper that murmured like the sea, but spoke no human tongue.

"Run! Fight!" Worm gibbered; but it did neither. Worm stayed, limping aimless circles on missing legs. "Help! Help! Help!"

"Marandu!" Paul cried.

The slim Jillan-body shuddered, once. "I will take you in," Marandu said. "Partitioned—I can't—"

Jillan-shape broke apart in shimmer. A larger glow appeared, folded about them, an order, a structure, a body vaster than their own.

Worm was in it, snuffling.

Move, the impulse came, or something very like the command to legs and limbs.

"Go with it," Rafe tried to say, at least he willed himself to say. He could stretch very far if he wished: or that was Marandu's thought.

$<>$ *was dying.* $<>$ *knew distress at that. The crew had already passed.* "Ship," $<>$ *said, tried to say, "go home."*

But Ship could not/would not hear. The Collective had betrayed $<>$, *implanting instructions* $<>$ *could not override.*

$<>$ *died and remembered it when* $<>$ *woke, with Ship long underway.*

FIND. REPORT. $<>$ *obeyed, until* $<>$ *had calculated that transmission scatter was too much, and the years too many, and nothing mattered any more but* $<>$*self.*

$<>$ *traveled. It was all* $<>$ *had left.*

$<>$ *made* $<>$*self for company.* $<>$ *sought other goals.*

$<>$ *took on passengers.*

He/they/she and Worm . . . participated in a body that had more limbs than they had collectively. They were old; and badly scared; and knew too much.

They/$<\wedge>$ *were victims of* $<>$*self, helpless in their voyage. Passengers multiplied.* $<>$ *took them in.* $<>$ *changed and grew complex and made other selves.*

$<\wedge>$ *shuddered, gazing at* $</>$ *in memory.*

But one of $<\wedge>$'s new-gained segments was of different mind.

Ship, he thought, with vast, vast desire. He was structure; Paul was complexity; and Jillan—Jillan was going at that thing, possessed for once of strength and size and a wrath stored up for years.

</ > swooped and struck.

They/Marandu moved, lancing through the patterns of the ship, darting this way and that at transmission speed, being here and there with electron lunacy.

"*Aiiiiiieeee!*" Worm wailed, and discovered <(((Λthem)))>self alive, to ((()))'s total startlement. "*Aiiii-ya!*"

</ > was in pursuit, was on them, through them.

"Hate you," one thing said, collectively; Cannibal was tangled with it and it lusted, that was all that filled its mind.

Fargone docks—

And They/Marandu/Worm; no-failure, not-now—beyond clear thought, beyond reasoning, except that they were still alive, like Worm, who had been a pilot once, and hurled ((()))'s skill into their evasions in the patterns.

"*Aiiiieeeiiiiii!*" Worm cried, going to the attack.

A red world lay in Marandu's past, much loved betrayer—for that memory, Marandu fought. "*Lindy!*" Rafe yelled, and felt Jillan and Paul distinctly at his side. Their own focus was a little ship, a hope, pilot-skill and stubbornness . . . no world to love at all, only Fargone's hell.

"*Aiiiiieeeeeeyaaa!*"

A wall loomed up at them, Rafe-face amid it, howling as they merged.

< > was amazed.

Bravery, <▵> had said. It was.

< > moved, with that same electron-swiftness as </ > took <▵> in.

< > dived after, rummaged through almost-congruencies, started ripping things into order in </ >'s distorted substance.

Merged—with < >'s own mad self; and <▵>; and sucked up disordered bits of other things.

Worm—retreated, whimpering.

Cannibal fled, outclassed.

Only Paul One stood, howling rage at < >.

And two others of itself surrounded it, denying divisions.

Two more joined with Rafe-mind, such of it as remained. It clung to them.

One cast herself amid it all, discovering loyalties beyond herself. Her double chose another target.

<∧> rode this last particle, straight to </>'s heart.

<<<∧/they ++>>> became <<∧they>>.

Became <<∧>>.

Then <>.

A shock went through the ship, a long silence.

Something very old had passed.

The passengers began at last to move. Certain ones fled for different refuges, old alignments having become impolitic, unsafe.

Worm danced, quite solemnly, for ((())) had gained a name. ((())) had become like Kepta in this, even if ((())) was Worm. ((())) had regained sanity; and pride; and glared from ((()))'s five eyes at Cannibal, who found it safer to retreat.

[] fled, precipitate.

<∗> shivered, in deep mourning for <∧>; for <∧> had remembered <∧>'s savagery at the last, and become quite sane.

< > stretched throughout the ship-body, taking all territories, all systems.

Trishanamarandu-kepta came to fullest awareness, and looked about < >'s surroundings as < > had when < >'s voyage began.

And at what < > had retained within-the-shell. That too.

Rafe put out his hands in the dark. His fingers met the extended arms, hard metal, rigid. He tried to feel his way backward amid this maze. Razor steel sliced his back in more places than one. His questing hands met the same no matter where he turned.

"Kepta," he said aloud, quite calmly; "Kepta—" Patiently. "I want the light back, Kepta; at least give me the light."

Kepta might have lost; might have won; the blades might start to move of a sudden and dice him down to something disposable.

"I want the light!" he cried.

Light blazed. He jerked, hit his back and arm against the knives and froze at the sting of wounds. The glittering arms were starkly poised about him, a web of razor steel and claws.

Rafe-shape phased in. "I've won," it said.

"Who—won?"

"Kepta. Me."

"*Which* of you?"

"Ah. Marandu told you." Rafe/Kepta moved through the metal arms, through the razors, coming clear to view. "The original. Myself. The one who brought you here."

"Either of you could have done that."

"Either would be me. But both my copies are gone, dissipated."

"Keep away from me!" And—*Either would be me*—sank in. He stared at it, finding the razor points at his back more comforting than its presence.

"Anxious still? It's your doing, you know: all three of you. Yourself, for instance—It never could quite break you down, not while Paul was there. Not while there was any vestige of him. That's your secret, your one secret. Responsibility. My double worked so hard keeping you alive. Mistake. And Paul: Paul One always trusted reason: and he couldn't withstand it when he met it face to face in Jillan; he couldn't bear that—or her solitude."

"Where are they? Are they all right?"

"Jillan, now," it said, inexorable. "Jillan was the crux. Marandu knew. She gave him—sanity. He was once very fierce—Marandu was, in certain causes. He'd forgotten all of them. And Worm—they called him Worm—he has affinity for you: nibbled up a bit of you, in your other form, as if he'd found one of his own missing bits."

"Kepta—where are they?"

Rafe/Kepta's face showed—it seemed—disappointment in him. A ghostly hand lifted, motioned to the center of the place, among the arms. "Come on, Rafe. Lie down. You'll sleep now. I'll keep my promise. We'll go to Paradise."

"*Where are they?*"

"I had to erase them, Rafe. I had no choice."

"*You*—" He dodged past the arms, the blades, half-blind.

Snick-snick—Arms moved in unison. Clamps seized his limbs and held, irresistible.

"Damaged," Kepta said. "They were irrevocably changed. What would you have wanted me to do?"

Rafe wept. He shut his eyes and turned his head; it was all the movement left him.

"I'll bring them back," Kepta said.

"Damn you—" He rolled back his head, heaved uselessly against the unflexing arms. The strength went out of him. Resistance did, and gathered itself up again.

"They'll be new again," Kepta said. "You understand. What happened to them—won't ever have happened—to *them*. The templates are clean of that. I do have charity." The arms clattered and retracted, *snick!* "You can harm them, far more than I ever could. Do you understand that?"

"No," he protested—everything.

"Not make them again?"

He wiped his eyes, hung there, his arms about the metal limb. It was cold. There was, for him, sensation; heat and cold; touch, taste; all the range of senses. "For what?" he asked. "What do you make them for in the first place?"

"Should I not?"

"You talk—" He caught his breath, caught his balance, straightened and walked over to sit on the smooth plastic bed amid the humps, the nodes, in the shining forest of the limbs, where it wanted him. "You talk about Paradise. Leaving me there. Forget that. I'm not leaving them to you, to make into what you want. Take me with them. Hear?"

"They'd object," Kepta said. "I know them very well."

"Damn you." He shuddered, lifted up his arm, flesh and bone. "You want to strip me down to what they are? Do that. At least I could touch them then."

"But you can. You already have. You're not thinking straight. Don't you know one Rafe-template's *you?* In every respect—he's you. You've already had your wish. He can touch them; be touched; touch *me;* do all the things you'd do. Dead, alive—that makes no difference. The only decisions are selfish ones."

He wiped his eyes a second time, bleak and blank and knowing insanest truth.

"Think about it," Kepta said. "There are choices."

"What am I leaving them to? Where are you taking them?"

"Vega, maybe; you mentioned that. Altair. They interest me. Places that have names—are so rare in the universe."

He looked at the doppelganger. His pulse picked up with hate. "Truth, Kepta. Once, the truth."

"Motives—"

"—won't make sense. *Make* them make sense. I want to know."

"Say that I travel," Kepta said. "And they will."

"For *what?*"

"Don't we all," asked Kepta, "travel? Who asks why?"

"I do."

"That is worth asking, isn't it? We are kindred souls, Rafe Murray."

"Don't play games with me!"

"I know. There's pain. I never promised you there wouldn't be. I never promised them. Do you want them back? Now?"

He was paralyzed, yes and no and loneliness swollen tight within his throat. He shook his head, found nothing clear.

"No choice is permanent. Except your first one. Will you go to Paradise?"

"I don't know," he said hoarsely. It included all there was. "Can I talk to them?"

"You said it to me, didn't you—they're not toys."

He dropped his head into his hands. "Don't do this to me."

"I only asked for choice."

"What if I ask you to wipe them out here? Off this ship. Out of this. Would you do that?"

"No," Kepta said. "Their templates would exist. I'd use them. Eventually."

"Honesty."

"Would it be—what they would choose?"

He sat and shivered until it seemed Kepta must lose patience and go away; but Kepta stayed, waiting, waiting.

"I want to be with them," Rafe said at last, so softly his voice broke. "Make me one of them."

"You don't understand," Kepta said. "Even yet."

"But I do," Rafe said. He swung his feet up and lay down on the machinery, blinked at the lights, the metal glare of knives. "I won't go. I won't leave them. Wake us up together, Kepta."

For a long moment Kepta stood. The cold seeped in.

"Yes," Kepta said. "I know."

Vega shone.

"No human's ever been here," Rafe said, confronting that white, white glare, that dire A-class star that no human would find hospitable. He felt its wind, heard its voice spitting energy to the dark. Ship had invented sensors for them, human-range.

"*Look* at that," said Jillan; and passengers hovered near, delighted in the four human-shapes, in new senses, in mindsets both blithe and fierce.

"Let ((())) try!" said Worm, who looked through human eyes, and shrieked and fled.

" " " crept out of hiding, as many had, who had been long reclusive. The timid of the ship had appeared out of its deepest recesses, now that $</>$ was gone.

"Look your fill," said $<>$. "There's time."

Paul just stared, arm in arm with Jillan-shape. Rafe and Rafe Two stood on either side. They kept their shapes, unlike some. They kept to their own senses exclusively, quite stubborn on that point.

"We're human," Rafe insisted. "Thank you, no help, Kepta. We don't make part of any whole."

Perhaps, Rafe thought, for he could still see human space, perhaps Kepta had betrayed him after all. Perhaps he had waked back there too, in a capsule near a much smaller star.

He hoped that he had not. He dreaded its loneliness.

"It was crazy," Rafe Two had said when they had waked together in the dark. "Rafe, you didn't have to."

"Come on," he had said then, in that dark place where they waked. "Sure I had to. I'd miss you. Wouldn't I? Maybe I do, somewhere. At Paradise."

Shapes crept close to them, hovered near.

Worm snuggled close, ineffably content.

It was a small, very old ship that *Hammon* found adrift.

"Something . . . 24," the vid tech deciphered the pitted lettering. "The rest is gone."

"God," someone said, from elsewhere on the bridge. "That small a ship—How'd she get out here?"

"Drifted," *Hammon*'s captain said. "Out of some system."

And later, with the actinic glare of suit-lights lighting up the